An Unwavering Desire !

An Unwavering Desire !

SUSHEEL KUMAR BATRA

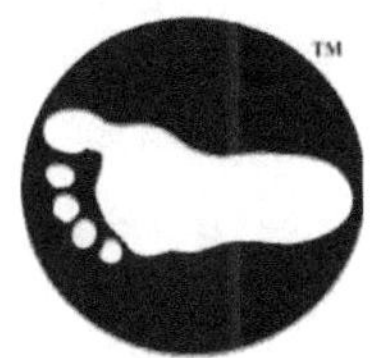

Bigfoot Publications

Because, there's a writer in everyone.

Published by

Bigfoot06 Publications (OPC) Pvt. Ltd.

211, Muzaffra, Sherpur, Pataudi, Gurgaon, Haryana (122502)

Website: www.bigfootpublications.in

Email: info@bigfootpublications.com

First Edition: SEPTEMBER 2022
ISBN: 978-93-90925-37-7

Printed in India

Dedicated to my Parents, whose memories always inspire me for doing something useful for our society & also for the aspiring youth of India.

$\mathbf{A}$cknowledgment

While writing the revised version of the literary fiction Aspirations now titled 'An Unwavering Desire', I consulted very frequently with my family members and now the result is in your hands. So, I thank my wife Shashi, son Puneet, daughter-in-law Swati, daughter Annie and son-in-law Gaurav.

I thank my granddaughter Sia who is now grown up and helped me in reading the book thoroughly and got its continuity corrected at certain times.

I am a bit confused, and the reason is how to thank my granddaughter Arshia and grandson Advik whose wonderful talks, intelligence, and smiling faces have inspired me to write enthusiastically.

Table of Contents

Prologue

When Karan with his wife Reena and daughter Sia entered the hall of Nath's farmhouse, they were delighted to see both grandma and granduncle sipping their tea. Sia ran towards Gayatri Devi, and all met happily. Karan looked around, and asked, "Where are Vinod and Archana?"

"They have gone to Lucknow to meet their parents," Premnath replied.

After enjoying tea with the elders, Karan took his grandmother's permission to go to Mukherji's house. He told her that Reena would staywith her parents, whereas he is planning to come back after dinner.

On Saturday morning when Karan was having breakfast with his grandmother and granduncle, Gayatri said suddenly to him, "Dear Karan please do me a favor, due to my bandage," she looked at her leg that had a bandage due to her fall last week on an uneven garden patch while on her brisk morning walk, "I don't want to go to Sagar's this afternoon for the birthday function of their younger grandson. Please go there with Sia and Reena. If yes, then I would inform Mrs. Sagar on the phone."

Karan smiled and said, "Do you know Grandma? You asked me for the same about six years ago."

"I don't recollect. Have you gone there for a birthday party?"

"Yes Grandma, I think that time you had some backache."

"As we regularly attend their functions, so I want somebody

from the family to attend."

I will check with Reena and then confirm the same to you." In the next 10 minutes, Karan confirmed with his grandmother about his attending the birthday party along with Reena and Sia.

On this, Premnath reacted happily, "Thank God I have been saved from attending it." The other two laughed vigorously.

When the breakfast was over, Premnath and Karan started inquiring about the latest progress of each others' professional pursuits.

Premnath's third book was published in 2004 which was about the latest trends in architectural development taking account of ecological balance. The book was the need of the hour and became an instant hit among laymen and it particularly attracted those who were against the haphazard development of urban infrastructure. Gayatri after speaking with Mrs. Sagar on phone briefed Karan, "They are starting the program quite early at 4 pm. So be there in time."

"Fine Grandma, it will be good. We will be free quite early from there.

Now I would like to go upstairs to the library and do not intend to have any lunch. I stopped eating lunch on holidays while at home."

"I will ask Shobha to send you some drinks & fruits."

Premnath already showed his inclination of going to his laboratory so both the men parted. Karan went to the library and took a book of his choice from the book rack to read. But his mind started wandering to those old memories when he saw Reena for the first time and after a few days' gaps, he could meet her at Sagar's grandson's birthday party. That day again at her grandmother's request, he recalled all the old memories of those days when he was quite involved in his love with Reena and what he heard in those days about Vinod's love story personally from him.

CHAPTER 1

Karan could not divert his attention from the girl. His eyes fell repeatedly on her face. He had seen her a few days ago when she was leaving the bookshop and he was just entering it. Karan could only get a glimpse of her because the moment he entered the shop, the owner greeted him, and he had to reciprocate. It was just impossible for him to go back immediately to take another look, but her face stuck in his mind.

One morning Karan's grandmother said, "There's an invitation from the Sagars' family for their grandson's birthday and, you know, dear, due to my backache I can't move, so please attend the function in my place." She further informed Karan that she had already told her friend, Mrs. Sagar that he would come. Karan did not respond. He was generally reluctant to attend such parties, but then he preferred to keep quiet for the time being. He knew his grandmother was friendly with Mrs. Sagar and could not go to the party only because of pain in her back. Otherwise, she enjoyed going to parties, as she was always the center of attraction, not only due to her personality but also because she always took an interest in solving other people's problems. After further deliberation, Karan felt that someone from the family ought to attend the function.

Karan's granduncle, Premnath, was also normally not interested in such parties, as these were a regular feature in the cluster of farmhouses where they were living. He agreed to go to them only to accompany his sister, Gayatri Devi, Karan's grandmother. He much preferred attending to his hobbies of gardening, experimenting with plants, or writing on the subject.

Karan's grandmother was in her late sixties and his granduncle was about six years younger. Premnath had been living in the farmhouse since the 1980s and Gayatri Devi had joined him about ten years ago.

Karan moved into the farmhouse about a year ago. He came there at the insistence of his granduncle and grandmother. He had always been a favorite with them and they loved him dearly. When Karan got his first job with a multinational management consultancy company, Prime-Mover, he had to commute to Bhikaji Cama Place, where the office was located. Both of them asked him to stay at the farmhouse, as it was closer to his office than his parent's home at Ashok Vihar. He used to visit his parents regularly at Ashok Vihar during the weekends.

Karan decided to go to the birthday party. When he arrived at the venue of the function, he suddenly got a glimpse of the same girl who was continuously disturbing his mind from the day his eyes fell on her. With some efforts, he found a proper site from where he could watch her undisturbed and within no time, he was engrossed in watching her. It was the same face he had seen at the bookshop. The girl was wearing Salwar-Kameez, the typical Punjabi suit, and had no makeup worth mentioning.

Karan had seen many beautiful girls at the University campus and around Delhi. Some were simple and the others were fashionable, but the girl his eyes were fixed on had a direct impact on his heart. The party was in full swing, with people of different age groups present, along with many children.

They had converted one corner of the hall into a dance area and pleasant, light music could be heard. A few young people and some of the children were dancing to the popular, fast music. Others participated by thumping their feet to the music or chatting. It was a large hall and there were at least two hundred people present. Mr. and Mrs. Prem Sagar were a very active couple who mixed with everyone at the party. It was the eighth birthday of their grandson Saptak, who lived with his parents in Mumbai. Saptak's parents were on a visit to Delhi at present. All these details entered Karan's mind and faded. His focus was on that face. Everything else was a blurred picture. Suddenly he heard Mrs. Sagar asking him, "How is your grandmother?"

"She is better, but her back pain persists."

"I really wanted her to come, but it is so nice of you to come in her place.'She then asked him if he needed anything and on his assurance that he was quite comfortable and would take care of himself, he found himself free from the hospitality of the old lady. He looked for the face with a bit of anxiety, wondering if he had lost her again, as he had the other day. He finally found her and started staring at her again, being a little more alert to ensure she stayed within his sight.

An announcement that the cake was to be cut was made and people started gathering around the table where the cake was placed. The birthday boy, who was busy playing with the other children, was called. Karan saw a good opportunity to stand near the girl who was also in the crowd around the table. As soon as the birthday boy cut the cake, everyone clapped and called out, 'Happy birthday Saptak'. Karan joined the others in wishing the boy.

The guests were now invited to partake in a variety of snacks placed on a few tables on one side of the hall. While Karan was picking up a plate, he sensed the same girl behind him. He offered her a plate and took another for himself. She thanked him and accepted the plate. Karan took a few snacks and sat around at an empty table. The girl served herself and came towards him, looking at the dance floor where dancing had restarted. Karan offered her a chair, which she accepted with grace, and slowly started eating. Karan could not bear that silence and attempted speaking, "I am Karan; I live near by at the Nath farmhouse."

"Do you!" She exclaimed with amazement and continued, "I also live next door at Mukherji's farmhouse. My name is Reena." Now it was Karan's turn to receive a pleasant surprise. He could not believe that she was the same girl who lived in his neighborhood.

"Are you Mr. Subodh Mukherji's daughter?" he asked. "I have never seen you before except..." He could not complete his sentence, and just sat there looking at her.

"I am not the daughter of Mr. Subodh Mukherji. I am his niece. My father, Mr. Subhash Mukherji, is his younger brother. He was a diplomat, and after taking voluntary retirement, we returned to India and settled down at the farmhouse."

Mesmerized Karan just listened to her. After coming out of his spell he spoke, "So at present, you and your family live with your uncle?"

Reena clarified the situation, "There are two adjacent buildings inside. This farmhouse belonged to my grandfather who expired a few years ago. We live on our side of the building."

Karan thought he should tell her a few things about himself, so he said, "Well I stay with my grandmother, Mrs. Gyatri Devi, and granduncle, Mr. Premnath. My parents live at Ashok Vihar in Delhi. After I completed my MBA, I got a job at Bhikaji Cama Place, which is closer to the farmhouse, so I have been staying here for more than a year. What do you do? Are you a student?"

She replied in the positive and then explained, "I did my graduation in Canada where my father was last posted. Now I intend to join a master's degree in French at JNU if I get admission."

On hearing that, Karan's eyes shone as the thought flashed through his mind that there was a scope of their meeting again and with this thought, he parted from her when the party was over. Reena got into her car and Karan kicked his motorbike in a dreamy way, reaching his farmhouse within five minutes.

When Karan returned, he told his grandmother everything about the party except his meeting with Reena. While giving her all the details in which she was interested, he was still feeling dreamy and wanted to go to his room to think about Reena. Since he was finding it difficult to tell his grandmother about the party without mentioning her, he made some excuse and went to his room as soon as he found the opportunity.

He sat on an easy chair near the window looking out. The light was dim, darkness was setting in, and he sat there just daydreaming about his newfound neighbor. He informed his grandmother through the intercom that he would not come down for dinner as he had eaten enough at the party. The serving boy, Sheru, brought him a glass of milk later at night. Karan asked him to put it on the table. He was not in a mood to talk, as was the daily routine with Sheru. Karan would normally ask him to sit down and inquired about him and the well-being of the other staff. Sheru felt self-important about this. He was always eager to tell him about the woes of the people working in the farmhouse. Karan would listen, not to gossip, but because he sincerely tried to help these humble people in the best possible way he could. Even today, he tried to control his mood; and asked Sheru to sit down and listened to him very patiently. When Sheru left, he gulped the milk, brushed his teeth, and strolled to his bed.

CHAPTER 2

Karan finished the day's work in the evening and looked at his watch. It was six o'clock. He said goodbye to his boss, Mr. Juneja, and left the office. He got onto his bike and hurried towards the bookshop in South Extension, to check the latest arrivals in the bookstore. In Delhi, the monsoon normally starts at the end of June, so the weather was quite pleasant, as it had rained for about two hours in the afternoon. The sky was clear while Karan was riding onto his bike and the cool wind was blowing. It was the onset of the month of Shravan (July/August), according to the Hindu calendar, which is also considered the month of romance. Most of the time, during this month the sky remains cloudy, with cool winds blowing all day, providing very pleasant weather. The atmosphere is charged with the songs of colorful birds.

Karan's mind was wandering between his search for a good book and a possible meeting with Reena, the latter being the more dominant desire. He expected her to be at the bookshop and daydreamed about the possible scenario when both of them could pour out their feelings from the depths of their hearts. He smiled at his wishful thinking.

When Karan entered the bookshop, his eyes fell on a book whose title attracted him. It was about India. He was so impressed by the little blurb that was written on the back cover, that he decided to buy it. As he was coming out of the bookshop, he saw Reena rushing towards it. "Hi Reena!" He called. She flashed him a smile and came towards him. Karan was so perplexed as if he had nothing to say to her but after a few awkward moments, he said, "Hello, how are you?"

"I am fine. How are you and what are you doing here?" He told her he came regularly to the bookshop to look for new arrivals.

Reena had come to pick up the latest magazines. After exchanging a few more words, both entered the bookshop. It was Karan's second visit to the shop but his emotions were quite different this time. Reena bought some magazines, and they came out of the shop, Karan asked her if she would like to have a cup of coffee. She replied, "Karan can it be some other day, I am late today." As he did not want to miss another opportunity to be with her, he nodded agreeably, and she left.

He continued watching her with dreams in his eyes till she was out of sight.

That night Karan intended to read the book he had bought, but the impressions of Reena's meeting were so overwhelming in his mind, that, he could neither read nor sleep properly. In fact, it looked as if his restlessness was his only means of passing his time.

The next day was so busy for Karan in the office that he had virtually no time to think about Reena as some important clients had come in and presentations were to be made, in which he was participating predominantly with Mr. Juneja. That evening, he returned straight to the farmhouse. After exchanging pleasantries with his grandmother, he went up to his bedroom to read the book; picked up the same, and sat near the front window. Thoughts about Reena started flashing in his mind once again. However, he felt contented thinking about meeting her the next day and diverted his attention successfully to the book at hand. After reading it for some time he placed the book on the table in front of him. The words of one particular paragraph was repeating again and again in his mind which were.

"India is a well-diversified country with all types of weather conditions. Its winters are cold but sunny. On the other hand, its summers are followed by monsoons. Its spring seasons have all the shades of green with beautiful blossoms of innumerable varieties. Its autumn season sees the fall of leaves of thousands of different plants, giving an impression of paradise. But a vast majority of the Indian population cannot enjoy this

spectrum of weather due to poverty. Each change in weather brings them its own hardships, as they are not equipped with the necessities to face these changes. Rains bring to them floods; the hot weather brings sunstrokes; the winter brings bitter cold in the form of diseases as they live in unprotected places without any shelter worth mentioning!

That paragraph led him to further thinking. The first question that came to his mind was: Who was responsible for the miserable conditions of about a quarter of India's population? India was one of the richest countries in the world in the ancient days. What went wrong? Could it be foreign domination?

Which was, of course, not for a small period. It lasted for over a thousand years during which India suffered not only financially but also culturally. There were only short periods during which India had very few genuine rulers when the people had some respite. Even when the foreign domination was over in 1947, the poverty of its people continued. Who was then responsible for the perpetuation of the misery of such a vast number of people even after more than half a century of independence?

Karan initially felt there was tardy development in comparison to the increase in population after the country's independence, but that reason did not satisfy him for the perpetuation of this sorry situation. The real responsibility he considered lay with corrupt political leaders, public servants, and businessmen, who looted the country with both hands. There was such a sordid nexus between them, that a few honest people from among them could not make much difference to a lot of the millions of poor in this country.

Karan's thinking was interrupted when he suddenly saw the clock on the wall. It was time for dinner so he hurried to the dining hall realizing his elders would have been waiting for him Karan found his grandmother, granduncle, and Vinod Sharma, Premnath's private secretary and manager of the farmhouse, seated around the dining table. Vinod lived in the farmhouse like any other member of the family.

Karan wished both his elders, said hello to Vinod, and excused himself, "I am sorry I am late." As he sat down,

Premnath smiled and said, "Dear, you are well in time."

While eating dinner, they spoke about the fine weather and their day's activities. After dinner, Karan had four rounds of the farmhouse with Vinod and then retired to his room.

The day to meet Reena arrived. There was a doubt in Karan's mind that she might not come. As he was completing his work, he felt an aching sensation and her face kept creeping into his mind. He was in a state of near delirium ever since he met her and felt romantically inclined towards her. He was a bit surprised about his feelings but was not in any mood to resist them; on the contrary, he was giving in to them.

Karan reached the bookshop on time and within a few minutes, he saw Reena coming out of her car towards him. He parked his bike and after wishing each other, both entered a restaurant near by. The restaurant was nicely decorated, with well-laid tables and chairs. Karan led her to a corner table, and he sat opposite her. A waiter took their order. Karan was in such a state of mind that it was difficult for him to think clearly. The same girl whose face had enchanted him was sitting just opposite him. The very girl who had created such strange sensations in him from the day he had her first glimpse. He could not decide whether it was love at the first sight or just an infatuation for a beautiful girl. He was even unsure that he was sitting opposite her. He was so engrossed with his thoughts that as if he suddenly became alive when he heard Reena's voice saying, "Karan, what's the matter with you? You don't seem well." He tried to put up a brave face and asked her, "What happened to your admission to JNU?" It was an innocent tactic to divert the topic as well as to find out the possibilities of their future meetings.

"I applied yesterday and will get the reply next week. The session starts in the third week of August." The waiter served them and while Reena was putting sugar into both cups of coffee, Karan felt as if he was seeing her properly for the first time. He saw a fair complexioned, round face with big, intelligent eyes, a beautiful, attractive nose, and long, silky hair. When she handed him his coffee, he suddenly came back to himself and asked, "You have lived in several countries, tell me whether your experience there was different than in India.

"I think living conditions in India and the countries where I have stayed are quite different. Not only that here in India people's outlook is quite differenton several issues. That does not mean that everything in India is bad.

There are certain very appreciative things one looks around. So, it's a mixed bag."

"I also think so. We seem to be like-minded on such issues which concern our country. I sometimes think so much has been happening in India in the last few centuries. The people suffered a lot, but still everything is not lost. A lot of goodness remains."

'Well, I have not so clear picture of Indian history, even then what you say seems correct. Karan, I would like to know more about my country. I hope you will be able to help me."

"You seem to be quite knowledgeable. Even then, if you like to listen to my imperfect assessment concerning our country which included its historical background also, I would happily like to tell you." Karan said laughingly.

After about an hour she said, "Let's move now otherwise I will be late." Karan immediately called the waiter, paid the bill and they moved out of the restaurant. Reena had to pick up her house maid, Luxmi, who had gone to meet her sister in Motibagh. Karan was following Reena's car and when she stopped at Motibagh to collect Luxmi, who was waiting for her, Karan stopped his bike at a distance. They entered the farmhouse cluster and went to their respective places.

On another day, Karan came out of his office to stroll during the lunch break and was walking around. The weather was cloudy, and he was in a good mood. It was only a day before yesterday since he had met Reena, but it seemed like ages to him. He was thinking about their last meeting and had just walked about a hundred meters from the office when he saw Reena sitting in a car parked along side. He went towards her and said with a bit of excitement, "Oh, a pleasant surprise! What did bring you here?"

She gave him a smile and replied, "Well my father had to go to the bankand as I was without much work at home, so I came along with him."

Karan observed now that the car was standing near a building housing a bank. He pointed toward his office building and said, "My office is in that building. It's the lunch break just now and the fine weather prompted me to come out for a walk."

Karan in fact wanted to convey that the weather was quite romantic, but in his speech, he was rather distant and mature and kept his emotions to himself. Within himself, he felt very poetic in those days particularly without finding any way out for expressions. Then a thought flashed into his mind that, as if, Reena came intentionally there in expectation of him, but he could not verify his wild guess. Both exchanged other pleasantries until her father came out of the bank. When he came to the car, Reena introduced Karan, "Papa this is Karan who lives in the Nath's farmhouse and works in a consultancy firm here. We happened to meet at Sagars at their grandson's birthday party a few days ago."

"Well, it's pleasant to meet you." Subhash Mukherji, Reena's father said politely to Karan.

Karan made the gesture of *namaste* at which Reena's father extended his hand, shook his, and inquired, "How are you related to Mr. Nath and Mrs. Gayatri Devi?"

When Karan informed him, Reena's father promptly said, "Oh! You are the grandson of that grand lady. I know your grandmother and Mr. Nath very well. I met them at two parties last year when I was on a visit to India." And he continued, "Why don't you come for a cup of coffee at our farmhouse?"

"It will be a pleasure to visit," Karan replied enthusiastically.

"I will look forward," Mukherji replied and entered the car and drove off. Karan while coming back to his office, was dreaming about the time when he would become well acquainted with Reena's family and would be able to meet her as and when he desired.

On the way back Reena's father told her about the two parties where he had met Nath and Gayatri Devi, Karan's grandmother. He further told her that they were wonderful people and he really enjoyed their company. Reena realized that her father knew more about Karan's family than she did.

CHAPTER 3

When Karan entered the farmhouse that evening, he saw his grandmother and granduncle sitting on the lawn sipping tea, as there were still traces of sunlight. The head gardener, Mohan Lal, was sitting near his granduncle, attentively listening to him. Karan could easily guess that it was probably about the latest trends in gardening, which is what they usually discussed.

Karan went towards them and greeted his grandmother, granduncle, and Mohan Lal, a middle-aged man. His grandmother and granduncle responded warmly and Mohan Lal with enthusiasm. Karan had given him his due respect ever since his childhood. Mohan Lal had worked at the farmhouse for the last twenty years. When he had first arrived, he was a young, unmarried man. Now he was married with two children and lived on the farm in one of the staff quarters. Premnath had constructed six flats for the staff working at the farmhouse. These flats had all the basic amenities. Most rich people do not bother about the life and living standards of their domestic help. Premnath was quite different; he was a simple and gentle person and was very considerate towards the people working for him; he treated them as part of his extended family. He arranged for the education of all the children staying there and paid for the medical treatment of all of his staff. The result was obvious; they were always ready to do anything for him.

Gayatri Devi, on the other hand, was a strict disciplinarian as far as work at the farm was concerned. Although she too was considerate towards others, no one dared question her authority and the staff were very attentive in performing their responsibilities when she was around. She was a teacher by profession and had been a principal of a senior secondary school for ten years before retiring, about eight years ago. Karan, her sister, and their cousins used to visit the farmhouse regularly from their childhood. Even when their grandmother was not living there, he and his sister accompanied her during their school holidays.

Premnath always welcomed his sister, her children, and grandchildren open heartedly. He was more energetic in those days and insisted they visit him regularly. Premnath went to the USA one year after passing his degree in B.Arch. After graduation, he got a job with a renowned architect consultancy firm in Mumbai. An American architect was in Mumbai on an assignment with Premnath's firm. He noticed Premnath's work and recommended him to his firm in the USA, which then offered Premnath a job. This occurred during the 1960s when there were no restrictions for professional Indians to get working visas from the USA.

Premnath was the youngest in his family. He had one brother about ten years older than him. His brother, Ramnath, who settled in Mumbai after his marriage, was not particularly attached to the family from the start. He died in a plane crash twelve years ago. Prem and Gayatri were close to each other from childhood. Gayatri got married when she was seventeen years old and was studying in the intermediate class. Since a good marriage offer came from old family contacts, she married comparatively young. Deendyal Malhotra, Gayatri's husband, was a modern man who wanted his wife to complete her education. So Gayatri graduated and went on to do her M.A. and B.Ed., and got a job as a teacher.

Prem's parents were ordinary, middle-class people who lived at Paharganj near the New Delhi Railway Station when Premnath went to the US. Prem was regularly sending sufficient money to his parents from there. He visited them every alternate year and they would press him to get married, but he avoided it. Prem wanted to marry, but the girl he had in mind was his senior colleague's daughter. His senior was also a partner in the firm where Prem was working. He was impressed by Prem's talents and happily agreed to their marriage.

Prem sent air tickets to his parents, sister, brother, and brother-in-law to attend his wedding in the USA. Deendyal excused himself since he had to take care of the family during Gayatri Devi's absence, but all the others attended his marriage.

Premnath was offered a partnership in the architectural firm where he had established himself as a specialist in landscaping. He agreed as the firm was doing very good business. Luckily for him, that very year the firm got new orders worth a billion dollars from an MNC to set up landscaped offices in different cities in America, Canada, and Europe. His married life started with all enthusiasm and love. His wife, Suzie, gave birth to a beautiful daughter, Ami, within the first year of their marriage. Suzie started neglecting her daughter's day-to-day requirements, which resulted in differences between husband and wife. Prem continued with his marriage because of his daughter; he did not want her to have a stepfather or a stepmother. Ami did not keep very good health and died at the young age of five. It was a great shock and set back to Prem, who felt that Suzie's irresponsible attitude of not taking adequate care of their daughter was one of the main reasons that she did not survive.

After the tragic death of their daughter, husband and wife started living separately and after about seven years of married life, they mutually got a divorce. Prem started losing interest in living in the USA and further pursuing his carrier there, even though he was doing extremely well. He was recognized as an ace landscape architect. He was an artist by nature and an architect by profession, which made landscaping a natural choice in his career. After staying on for three more years, he came back to India permanently, at the age of about forty-three.

When he left, he received a lot of money from his partnership. He also disposed of all the immovable assets he had bought during his stay there and brought his money to India in the 80s. Premnath wanted to live a peaceful life so instead of starting a consultancy firm he just bought a farmhouse in the cluster of farmhouses, which was well planned and connected by a wide cemented road to the Mehrauli Road. He invested his remaining money in bonds, government securities, debentures, and shares of a few blue chip companies through a friend who was a chartered accountant and whose firm looked after investment business along with chartered accountancy work in Delhi.

Premnath settled down in the farmhouse with his parents. They had continued to stay at Paharganj refusing of shifting to a better locality like New Rajinder Nagar, despite Prem's repeated insistence from the USA. It was not a matter of money, because Premnath would have supported the move but they were unwilling to leave their old surroundings. Prem took good care of his parents. His sister Gayatri visited them at the farmhouse regularly. Prem would send his car to bring Gayatri or her family on weekends.

Premnath's father Kaidarnath Khurana expired about five years after moving to the farmhouse at the ripe age of eighty-three and his mother expired four years later, at about the same age. Premnath became lonely at the farmhouse. About one year after his mother's death, his brother-in-law died suddenly. Premnath thought about the possibility of his sister shifting to the farmhouse. He started persuading her to get premature retirement and move in with him, but Gayatri Devi refused. She did not want to leave her job before superannuation, as she was well respected in education circles. Her brother's pressure was ultimately too much to resist; moreover, there was much affection between the two. The major reason for shifting to the farmhouse was her transfer from Model Town to R.K. Puram

School, in South Delhi. That school was located closer to Nath's farmhouse than Ashok Vihar, where she stayed with her sons and their families. Premnath also offered her a car with a driver for commuting to and from school and finally, she decided to shift. She consulted both of her sons and daughters-in-law before shifting to his brother's house. All of them felt that the new arrangement was good for both the sister and the brother. Gayatri's children and grandchildren were fond of Premnath, who always showed them a lot of affection.

Gayatri Devi was a very active lady even at the age of fifty-eight. She looked ten years younger and had an impressive physique and fair complexion. She was a strict disciplinarian. Her school results were normally excellent and she got many awards during her career as a teacher, vice-principal, and principal. Premnath admired his sister's magnetic personality, which was internally soft but outwardly stern.

Gayatri Devi was a woman of principles, with a modern outlook, for which some credit goes to her husband, a follower of the Arya Samaj, a forward-looking Hindu sect. The family did not follow irrational social taboos nor did they perform irrelevant rituals. Deendyal was quite a fire brand and an upright person. His outlook affected Gayatri Devi, and she learned to see things from their proper perspective. Her personality was such, that people always felt her presence when she was around. She was intuitive, and noticed some change in her grandson, but could not make out the cause for it.

Prem was a regular visitor to the club but avoided parties, which were held with pomp and show. At the club, he preferred playing chess whereas at his farm he was absorbed in gardening, plant research, or writing. He won an award for the best farmhouse garden. Being an architect who specialized in landscaping, he could do wonders with his creative imagination. When he returned to India permanently, he was offered several high-ranking jobs from construction companies, renowned builders and architect consultancies, etc. but he was not interested in working just to make money. He thought he had sufficient funds to pursue his creative hobbies. He believed in the acumen of his friend, a chartered accountant, and invested his money through him. His contented nature paid him rich dividends in later years. He found sufficient time to write a book on landscaping, describing his experiences abroad. The book was very popular with the public and strangely enough, was also included as a textbook in landscaping architect courses. Despite these achievements of a popular book and a prestigious award with a hefty bank balance and good investments, he was quite humble and simple in his habits.

Nath's farm area was two-and-a-half acres. Most of the farms in the locality were of the same size. Mukherji's farm, where Reena lived, was of five acres area. So obviously it was twice as wide as Nath's. One half was exactly opposite Nath's. In fact, it was a combination of two adjacent farms, and the main building had two similar adjoining portions, built after getting special permission from the authorities. The cluster was located on the right of the Mehaurali Road when going towards Gurgaon with a common gate, a well-lit road connecting it to the main road, and twenty-four-hour security.

The entrance was quite close to *Andheria Mor*. Further down, on both sides of the road were about twenty other farmhouses with their own securities and entrances. The road, starting at the Mehaural Road end was fifty feet wide up to the fifth farmhouse. It was then widened to two hundred feet for the next two hundred and fifty feet and then back again to fifty feet. There was a raised circle in the center of the widened part, planted with grass and flowers. It was well styled and was built at the time the farmhouses were initially offered for sale. The owners of these farmhouses formed an association, which maintained the common entrance, security, lighting,

roads, etc. Nath's farmhouse was the fifth from the entry side of Mehaurali Road, and Mukherji's farmhouses were the fourth and fifth of the opposite side.

CHAPTER 4

Karan was five feet nine inches tall, fair complexioned, and well built with sharp features. He was by nature a socially conscious person. Even in his school days, he disliked the disparity prevailing all around him and he tended to side with the weak. He was always helping needy students or friends in whatever way he could. When Karan joined Delhi University, he came across some other students who had similar leanings. They made up a group of five and became good friends. As they were all doing their B.Sc. (Hons.) in the same subject, they studied, ate, played, and discussed things together most of the time. It was their view that the prevailing social set up left much to be desired. Karan had an unwavering desire to change the ills prevailing in society. One day they decided to start a club of like-minded people who would stick to the charter they were to prepare based on their experiences in their lives. They named the club 'Aspirations' through which they wanted to fulfill their aspirations. Those five friends, the founder members of the club were Karan, Vivek, Puneet, Sujeet Singh, and Rohan. They took an oath to follow certain principles. New members were accepted only if all the founder members would give their consent. Their regular fortnightly meetings took place at the University lawns, public parks, or their individual homes as deemed fit. These meetings normally lasted from morning until evening and they would have lunch together at some place nearby. After the launching of the club, Karan started a personal diary in which he wrote all the developments concerning the club and its members.

He wrote on its first page the five points on which they took an oath, which became their charter:

1. Not to accept dowry, being a social evil.

2. Not to accept bribes no matter whatsoever position is held.

3. Not to follow irrational social traditions blindly.

4. Not to give donations for religious activities unless those are verified for their proper use; Give money to help the needy and poor by making regular savings.

5. Not to follow fashionable trends blindly, only because they are new; accept them after thorough examination and discussion.

Their club had been running very successfully for the last six years. There were fifteen members, and all the members were following the five-rule charter quite religiously. During the current year, two of the founder members, Puneet and Sujeet, got married. Both refused to accept dowry.

Karan seemed to be happy with the performance of the club. They held their meetings once every two months now, as they were no longer students and all of them were working. One of the founder members, Vivek, joined the family business with his father and brother. Before joining, he made it clear to his father that he would follow the club charter as he very well knew that in a family business, one had to follow one's parents blindly in the matter of marriage, etc. Only after his father agreed to the conditions did he join, and the business was running very well from the day he joined it. Vivek was closest to Karan as a friend.

Karan was quite a liberal fellow except that he was strict about following the club charter, which was very close to his heart.

During their college days, the group of five visited a few places in India during their holidays. They had twin purposes for this. Firstly, they wanted to see the important places in their country, and secondly, they wanted to study the cultural backgrounds of different people. They also attended important social happenings in the city like exhibitions, dramas, public lectures by renowned personalities, acclaimed movies, etc. After graduation, they were separated. Puneet and Rohan joined a postgraduate course. After doing his M.Sc., Puneet cleared the U.G.C. examination and joined as a lecturer in a college at Delhi University. Rohan continued with his studies and was doing a Ph.D. Sujeet Singh appeared for the Civil Services examinations twice and was finally selected for the Allied Services as an Income Tax Officer, with his first posting luckily in Delhi, so currently, all Karan's close friends were in Delhi. Perhaps that was the reason that Karan, after completing his MBA from FMS, Delhi University, preferred to work at a lower salary in Delhi, even though he had received several better offers from outside Delhi. The MNC he joined had a name in consultancy services and it was well known in student circles that those who were bright got quick promotion in that company.

CHAPTER 5

Karan's closest friend Vivek was flourishing in his business. Vivek had a jovial nature and Karan enjoyed his company very much. In his present stateof mind, disturbed as he was due to his emotional involvement with Reena, he felt it best to talk to Vivek.

Normally Karan went to his parents at Ashok Vihar over the weekends, where he would meet other old friends also. He decided to meet Vivek before going to Ashok Vihar. Vivek lived at Lajpat Nagar, and his office was at Defence Colony. Karan fixed a meeting the day before, over the telephone. Vivek suggested meeting at the City Club where he was a member, and which was located near his office.

The building of City Club building was quite huge and was situated on the main road. There was a big lawn with a variety of beautiful flowers planted around and a few small fountains in front of it. Entry to the club was through a large glass door. It had six floors and four lifts. The reception counter was, as usual, near the entrance. Vivek, after making the entries in the visitors' register, went straight to the lift with Karan to go to the dining hall on the fourth floor. There were many round tables in the hall, covered with beautiful tablecloths. Each table had four chairs. They chose a vacant table near the front window. On the way to the table, Karan could see a billiard room on his right. There were a lot of people around. Vivek told him that club members came there with business clients during the lunch hour, not only to eat but also for some entertainment in the form of playing different indoor games.

As soon as both friends sat down, the waiter came for an order It was early and there were many vacant tables. Vivek gave an

. initial order of juice after consulting his friend.

Vivek had recently got engaged to a Chandigarh girl at a simple ceremony where only the rings were exchanged. His father cooperated with him as he had promised earlier. When Vivek was in the doldrums about joining his father's business, he had taken Karan into confidence, and on Karan's advice; he clarified his views with his father. Both of the friends had a lot of faith in each other.

Vivek asked his friend about the sudden meeting to which Karan replied, "I am a bit upset these days and wanted to discuss the matter with you."

"What has upset you?" There were clear signs of bewilderment on Vivk's face.

Karan took a deep breath and started telling his friend slowly about his first meeting with Reena at the bookshop and then at the birthday party. He also told him about the other meetings. After a pause, he informed him in a rather low tone that he could not sleep properly during the night and her image kept disturbing him several times during the daytime. Vivek gave a smile and spoke with intensity, "You are in love, and the one you are in love with seems to be interested in you also."

"It is not so simple. You say I am in love. All right, I agree but what about her? She may be responding in a friendly way or just being civil as I am her neighbor."

"Now I understand the reason for your disturbance. It is to know her mind. How she feels about you."

Karan immediately reacted, "Really *yaar (friend)*! It has clicked me too now. It seems so simple now. My mind is disturbed because I am desperate to know her mind; her feelings toward me. Thanks, Vivek, by just talking with you we could hit on the solution to the problem."

Vivek became his jovial self on seeing his friend's improved mood and changed the topic to cheer his friend further. He started making faces at a person who was sitting with a beautiful girl and looked as though he was trying to convince her about something, but was getting distracted by Vivek's facial expressions. On this Karan smiled, as he knew no one could stop Vivek from doing such things. It was good that the waiter came well in time for the lunch order.

Slowly the hall was filling up and soon all the tables were occupied. They could hear the light music. Both the friends had a lot of talks and relished their lunch. Vivek was quite satisfied to see his friend's calm face, now that they had discovered the reason for Karan's disturbed mind. While getting up, Karan thanked his friend again for resolving his issue. As they were leaving the dining hall, then they passed near the same couple and Vivek again made faces, looking the young man straight in the eye. He again lost his concentration and looked towards Vivek. The girl also got distracted and started looking at him. In the meantime, Karan who was a few feet behind his friend could see a sign of relief on the young man's face that Vivek was leaving the venue.

CHAPTER 6

Vijay Malhotra, Karan's father, lived in Ashok Vihar, a colony in North Delhi, with his wife, Kamini, in their own house. The late Deendyal Malhotra and his, wife Gayatri Devi, had purchased it. It was a double-storied house. Deendyal and Gayatri Devi lived on the ground floor, while Vijay Malhotra, his wife, Kamini, and their children occupied the first floor. It was a joint family set-up with one kitchen on the ground floor. A few months after the death of Gayatri's husband, her younger son, Ramesh, who was working with a private company in Bangalore, changed his job and started working in Delhi. At the same time, Gayatri was transferred to R.K. Puram.

Under the supervision of their mother, the elder brother shifted to the ground floor and the younger one moved into the first floor with his wife, Sunanda, and two young kids. A separate kitchen was established and within a few days, Gayatri shifted to her brother's farmhouse. Both the brothers and their families got on well together.

Vijay Malhotra was around fifty years old and was an engineer by profession. He was recently appointed a director in the Central Electricity Authority which was a Government of India Institution. At the start of his career, he served for about three years in DESU (Delhi Electric Supply Undertaking). Due to the rampant corruption prevailing in DESU, he applied through the UPSC for an assignment in the present organization and was selected as Assistant Director. He started enjoying his new job and new office where the main activities involved design and consultancy services.

Vijay's honesty influenced Karan's own outlook.

Vijay Malhotra was a man of simple habits. He used chartered bus facilities to commute to and from the office and kept his personal car for weekends and local use. A majority of private as well as government employees used chartered buses as office transportation in Delhi to avoid fatigue during rush hours. After the partition of India, Delhi became a populous city due to the migration of people from the part of undivided India now Pakistan. Later its population grew much faster than other Indian cities, as unemployed people in search of jobs from the surrounding states as well as from Orrisa (now Odisha), MP, Bihar, etc., flocked to Delhi in search of work. Since UP, the most populous state of India, is next door to Delhi, this also affected the population in Delhi. All this while, the Delhi Administrative Machinery slept shamelessly, like Kumbhkaran (the sleepy brother of Ravana). It was only in recent years when Delhi roads were converted into a continuous chain of speed-breakers did Kalyug Kumbhkaran woke up to construct flyovers and provide metro services.

Deendyal had become an Arya Samaj follower when he was a young married man. He along with his friend once when heard a swami giving a lecture on public ground. Both the friends were initiated into the Arya Samaj from that day onwards. Gayatri also went with her husband to hear a number of swamis who visited their area, either at the Arya Samaj or on public grounds, and was influenced by their progressive social thinking. She was particularly attracted to it because of its vigorous campaign to cleanse Hindu society from irrational customs, taboos, and rituals and its stress on removing the caste system and favoring mass education, particularly for women. Gayatri, being a teacher and a daring lady liked the ideals of the Arya-Samaj and followed its progressive outlook with great zeal without becoming an official functionary. Vijay Malhotra had imbibed his first lessons on anti-corruption and love for his country from his parents. His gurus were not swamis; they were his own parents. Karan took in the essence of the Arya Samaj without visiting it, but he had great respect for the wonderful work performed by it for the social restructuring of Hindu society.

31

CHAPTER 7

When Karan reached the gate of his house, he saw his sister, Mudra, coming from the other side of the road with books in her hands. He stopped at the gate and her sister rushed towards him full of excitement, her face was glowing with happiness. Karan showed his affection to his sister in the Indian way, and both inquiring about each other, entered the house. Karan guessed, "I think you are returning from your tuitions?"

"Yes, *Bhaiya* (brother) it was six hours of study at the academy."

The academy meant the tuition classes run by First Academy, which had been very popular among students for many years. Mudra was a brilliant student but these days it was almost compulsory to get private coaching for the tenth and twelfth classes due to cut-throat competition.

More over, the present examination system put a lot of pressure on the students in a very unhealthy way. The question was who would reform it. Everyone just succumbed to the system. It was felt that those who were at the helm of affairs were either helpless or not in the least interested in improving this social-cum-educational malady.

There was an urgent need for a visionary politician who would dare to change the rotten system along with opening better job opportunities so that the acute pressure on Indian students could be used constructively for their betterment instead of only cramming for competitions or short-term gains. As both sister and brother entered the lobby, Karan touched his mother's feet, the customary gesture of respect towards elders amongst Hindus.

Kamini embraced him and inquired, "How are you, my son? And how areboth *ma* and *mamaji* (maternal uncle)?"

"Both are well *Ma*. You were talking to them on the telephone only yesterday." Karan sat with his sister in the lobby discussing the daily routineof life while their mother went to the kitchen to arrange some cold drinks and snacks for both. Since it was a Saturday and a holiday, his father had gone out to meet a friend. He too entered the house, so Karan got up and touched his father's feet. On seeing his son, Vijay's face lit up with a broad smile.

The family atmosphere in India, in all categories of social set-ups, was always full of emotions. A family meant a joint or extended family and although affection was a dominant emotion, other emotions like anger, jealousy, and hatred also played their roles occasionally, making Indian life more, colorful than those of the west.

Karan went with Mudra to meet their uncle on the first floor. Although Mudra was quite busy with her studies these days, she liked to enjoy a few moments in her brother's company. Her final examinations for the twelfth standard were a few months away. Karan touched the feet of his uncle Ramesh and aunt Sunanda. Both reciprocated with a lot of affection by hugging him. Ramesh inquired, "How is life at your job and the farmhouse?"

"It is fine at both places. How is your job going on Sir?
You were thinking of changing."

"Well, I dropped the idea because the company is giving me my promotion which was overdue.

"Well, then, congratulations!"

"Thanks."

Both Karan's' cousins Winnie and Ishu, who met him with several hugs were now sitting on the arms of the sofa where Karan was sitting. They were making affectionate gestures towards him. Karan gave each of them a box of chocolates and one of the same lots he had already given to his sister earlier.

After dinner when Karan went to his bed, Reena's face came into his mind. He continued watching that face with his mind's eyes and then slept with contentment.

On Sunday Karan thought it best to meet a few of his friends living nearby. He selected two, and after breakfast, went off on his bike to meet them. They mused about the good old times, and he returned before lunchtime. All the members of his, as well as his uncle's family, had lunch together, laughing and cracking jokes with each other. He started his return journey around 4 p.m. after saying goodbye to everyone at Ashok Vihar.

As Karan's bike entered the gate of the farmhouse's cluster, he saw a car coming up and a female voice said, "Hello Karan! How are you?"

It was Reena's voice! Karan immediately looked at the car, which had justpassed him, and stopped. He saw Reena was in the driving seat. On her left, her maid and assistant Luxmi were seated.

Karan replied, "Hello Reena! Where are you coming from?"

"I went to the Green Park market for some shopping. What about you?"

"I am coming from Ashok Vihar after meeting my parents, sister, and uncle's family."

"Oh, I see. How are they?"

"Quite fine, thank you."

"You have not asked me about my admission."

"Oh sorry, what happened about your admission?"

"I got the admission."

"That's fantastic, so when can we celebrate?" "When we meet

next time, we will fix the time."

Reena started the car, which indicated that she was ready to go. She waved her hand while her car slowly moved ahead.

Karan smiled and watched her going ahead. He simultaneously felt joy and sadness. Joy because he met her and sadness as the meeting was so shortand the next meeting had not been fixed. Still, he was in a good mood, and when he entered his granduncle's farmhouse, he was whistling.

He went straight to his grandmother and embraced her with warmth. Karan did this very rarely; only when he was very happy. Normally he remains formal with his grandmother particularly as she remains that way, with her emotions always under control. Gayatri asked naturally, "Karan you seem to be very happy. What is the news? Will you share it withme?"

"Look Grandma today the weather is fine so along with the evening tea get something special made like *pakodas* (a popular Indian snack).

Gayatri immediately replied, "Why not my dear?" She instructed the cook on the intercom.

The sky was suddenly overcast with dark clouds within a few minutes. A cool wind started blowing. Karan's mind was in unison with the fine weather after meeting Reena, so his happiness seemed to collaborate with the weather.

Gayatri sent Sheru to inform Premnath to come for tea. While tea was served, with different varieties of *pakodas*, Prem joined the party. These days he remained very busy with gardening. The new plantation activities were mostly performed during the rainy season and proved very successful.

During that season he got a special variety of trees planted on the farm, which after a few years, would become beautiful trees full of flowers. The most interesting part of this, as explained by Premnath, was that beautiful flowers of different colors would bloom on the same tree. He was very enthusiastic about such plants. He also explained that he was planting at least fifty trees because the success rate of these plants developing into trees was quite low even when utmost care was taken. Premnath had ordered these plants from the Shivalik Range where he had gone last year and was dumb founded on seeing such a strange flowering tree. He had decided immediately that he would arrange to bring saplings of these trees to his farm. He talked to the local people and finalized with a responsible man of the area to send the saplings in a truck, which had arrived a few days ago.

Premnath was always collecting different varieties of plants from India's vast flora, and it made his farmhouse famous. Whenever the topic of plants came up, Prem always participated in the discussion with a lot of enthusiasm and with a child's curiosity.

After tea, Karan went to the library. It was not a room, but a big hall on the first floor, very well maintained, with racks full of books. There were windows on three sides of the hall so that while reading a book, one could also enjoy the beautiful greenery of the farmhouse. Karan always liked to spend a few hours there on holidays. The book he had bought a few days ago was now a part of the library, and since he had not completed it, he picked it up and soon got absorbed in reading.

In bed, that night, whatever he read during evening hours while sitting in the library was still going on in his mind and he started thinking about the historical period discussed in the book. In ancient days, from about 3000 BC to about 1000 AD in India, there was sufficient freedom of thought and women had enough importance. Their status in society was better than what it is even today! The fact was that India was more civilized at that time than most of the present-day countries and without the ills confronted by the industrialized nations.

When the country was under alien domination, a few foreign scholars realized the greatness of its mighty civilization. But alas! That mighty civilization was not ready to face the onslaughts of less civilized foreigners. The basic reason for this was perhaps India's gradual absorption of the concept of ahimsa (non-violence) due to its expanded level of consciousness, which became one of the main features of its civilization. Those who came to this land because of their lust for gold did not understand such great ideals due to their different upbringings. When it was known that other countries with different ideologies existed, it was utter folly for Indians not to be prepared to face foreign aggression with all their might. That attitude of not defending themselves with physical force was even wrongly misconstrued by a few of them as an act of non-violence and did India the uncalculated harm. Foreign rule of such a long duration destroyed the originality of thoughts, free expressions, and rich cultural values, and set our country back by centuries. Though it was a loss to all humanity, the visible result was that India became a country full of illiterates, having blind faith in superstitions, resulting in a very inferior social set-up.

Karan changed the time of the historical clock in his mind from a few thousand years to a few hundred years earlier and started thinking about the period when the British came to India. They had a very poor view of India except for its riches which had attracted them. A few learned Englishmen encountered the magnificent books written in Sanskrit during the last 5000 years (Particularly from about 3000 BC to 1000 AD). They, along with other learned Europeans, realized the greatness of India and in being Indian. Sanskrit, the ancient language, is a very scientific language.

Strangely it is concluded that it's the ideal language for computers, but with the existence of such a great language, the language of the conquerors took a firm base in India. Even after India became independent, English continues to remain the language of educated Indians along with Hindi and one of the rich Indian regional languages. It seems the continued preference for English as a language was perhaps due to its being the language of the lone superpower, the USA. The language of the foreigners started benefiting the country where it had come as the language of aggressors. Through English, India started dominating the computer software world as the Indian mathematical brain of the English-speaking educated classes was bringing in a lot of foreign money to India. Ultimately and interestingly, India started getting its due share. While thinking about all this, sleep engulfed Karan and he only woke up when the sun was high in the sky.

The next day was a holiday, but Karan went to his office as a meeting with a client had already been fixed. After the discussions on the new project with the client and his boss were over, he ate his lunch. Karan returned to the farmhouse early in the evening. The sky was getting cloudy again, even though it was nearing the end of the monsoon season. Karan went to the library after informing his grandmother of his arrival. He sat on an easy chair near the front window and started relaxing. A thunderstorm had begun, and he could hear heavy rainfall. He looked out of the window because he always enjoyed the rain. Within a few minutes, the rainfall subsided. He could see in front of him a rare combination of nature's beauty with the drizzle on the front lawn and the landscaped scenario with the wonderful flowering plants, which his granduncle had converted into a work of art. He could not help but appreciate his granduncle's high caliber.

CHAPTER-8

Premnath had written two books, one on home gardening and another on landscaping. Laymen, professionals, and critics appreciated both books. As his books were widely read, he received many letters, both from the ordinary readers and the learned. He was always very prompt in replying and for that, his deft secretary, Vinod Sharma, was a real boon to him. Vinod prepared the replies to ordinary readers himself. A man at the computer typed them and then they were then sent for Premnath's signature. Premnath used to reply the certain letters written by the specialists.

It was Vinod Sharma's seventh year as secretary to Premnath and manager of the farmhouse. Premnath had written his first book soon after he returned to India and settled down at the farmhouse. Due to the tremendous response to the book, he could not pay enough attention to his hobbies mainly gardening, and he felt the need to have a private secretary, who would look after his correspondence, catalog the books in the library and maintain the farmhouse. He found a person of such talent in the form of Gopichand Sharma who was a retired teacher. Premnath availed of the services of Gopichand for about eight years. Then due to his age, and his own strong recommendations, his nephew, Vinod Sharma replaced him. The management of the farm had increased manifold as it had slowly developed a plant laboratory. It had an office with modern facilities like a computer, fax machine, photocopier, etc. The staff salaries had to be disbursed and farm-related expenditures and account books had to be maintained.

Gopichand went to his hometown, Lucknow, to stay with his son. Premnath as per his liberal nature adequately compensated his retiring privatesecretary.

Vinod Sharma was a well-qualified, energetic young man and within a few days won over Prem's heart. He worked hard, was always prompt in action, and had a very cheerful nature. Vinod was given an assistant and if he had to go out for work, the staff car was available for use. Vinod often had to go out to liaise with government offices for water and electricity supply in case of disruptions and visit the chartered accountant quite frequently on behalf of Premnath. He needed to go to the market to buy things to keep the buildings and laboratory in excellent working condition and a number of other activities. Premnath was now free from the day-to-day requirements of the farmhouse and was completely engaged in his creative hobbies. Despite that, nothing was done without consulting him. Prem's investments were managed by his chartered accountant, Mr. Kapoor, who was his school friend. Regular contacts for the exchange of papers were done through Vinod, so Prem's visits to Kapoor's office were limited to only those where his personal presence was required, whereas their family visits to each other were comparatively more frequent.

Vinod Sharma was given accommodation in the main farmhouse building.

He was considered a part of the family and was asked to have dinner with the family or in his room only when not well or due to some other urgency.

Vinod did a one-year P.G. Diploma in computer applications after gettinghis B.Com. Both qualifications proved very useful in performing his job well. His computer knowledge especially, proved useful when Premnath wrote his second book.

Karan liked Vinod, especially his humorous nature, and tried to utilize his experiences, since he was older, by consulting him occasionally. Whenever he was in a low mood, Karan went to his room to listen to his witty remarks and see him copying the acting of film stars. He could not control the flood of laughter when watching him mimic them.

Vinod was five feet ten inches tall, with a fairish complexion. Being slim,he looked taller. No one, at any time could point to a shortcoming in his administration of the farm, which included the laboratory requirements.

Having grown up in Lucknow he brought with him a fascination with Urdu *Shayri* (A type of Urdu Poetry).

CHAPTER 9

On Saturday, as decided the previous week, Karan was at Vivek's house and intended to go on to his parent's home after meeting his friend.

Immediately on ringing the bell, Vivek came out as if he was waiting for him. Both friends embraced each other, entered the drawing-room, and sat on a sofa in one corner of the room.

Vivek said hurriedly, "What's the progress with Reena?"

Taking a deep breath Karan replied, "I met her on Sunday by chance on the way home, but there is no real progress."

On Vivek's insistence, Karan narrated the details of last Sunday's meeting. After listening carefully, he concluded, "At least you have tried and asked her for another meeting. I feel it's a good sign."

"You know I want to know her heart and at this stage, I can't ask her directly. I need several meetings, long meetings with her."

"You are on the right track now, as your line of action is clear to you."

"My mother is insisting me on seeing other girls for marriage as she is getting a lot of offers. She keeps asking me about it and when there is no reply from my side, she inquires whether I have already selected someone?"

Vivek smiled and said nothing.

Karan continued, "Without knowing Reena's heart, I simply have no reply to my mother's queries."

"If you really want to know her feelings about you then you

have to ask her directly as you don't know any of her friends."

"I can't just ask her directly until I develop greater intimacy. At present, I don't even have a date for our next meeting. Most of my meetings with her have happened by chance."

"Now you want to meet her and that too not by chance."

Vivek started thinking about it. In the meantime, the maid served tea and snacks. Looking at Vivek's face, it seemed clear that he was busy solving the puzzle and he came out with a solution as well.

"There is a possibility of your meeting Reena. I can request my *bhabhi* (sister-in-law) to talk to her on the phone and call her here."

Karan thought about that and felt happy his friend was atleast trying his best to help him. He finally said, "There should be a solid reason for *bhabhi* to call her."

Both of the friends started thinking about a solid reason for calling Reena.

Vivek came up with an idea, "You know the exhibition at Pragati Maidan started yesterday. Though it is not as big as the annual one in November, it is also multifaceted, covering many different items. You can invite her for it with *bhabhi's* help."

Inviting Reena to the exhibition was a good idea and it appealed to Karan. Moreover, he thought that Reena came to India only a few months ago and she might not have visited Pragati Maidan, a place worth visiting. It was alsoa coincidence that Vivek's *bhabhi*, Savita, was quite free with Karan. When it was agreed, Vivek went inside and came back after a few minutes accompanying his sister-in-law. Karan wished her and offered his seat as amark of respect.

Vivek explained the current issue to Savita and requested help by calling Reena. Savita immediately agreed. Karan had a visiting card, which Reena's father gave him when they met in front of the bank a few days ago. It also had their residence phone number. When Karan was desperate to meet Reena, he had thought of calling her but did not dare, in case she didn't like it, but he found no fault in Savita calling Reena. Karan dialed the number and gave the phone to Savita. When the phone was lifted at the other end, she said, "May I speak with Reena please."

"Sure, I'll just call her please wait. May I know who is on the line?"

"I am Savita." Reena came on the line and said, "Yes? I am Reena on theline."

"Hello Reena, I am Savita, the sister-in-law of Karan's friend Vivek.""I see. Good morning, what can I do for you?"

"Well Reena please speak to Karan," and Savita gave Karan the phone who said, "Hello Reena, it's Karan, how are you?" And he continued, "I am at my friend's house at Lajpat Nagar. We have made a program to visit the exhibition at Pragati Maidan. Both the place and the exhibition are worth seeing. There are three of us, myself, my friend Vivek, and his sister-in-law, who just spoke to you. Would you be interested in joining us? We will be free by about 6 p.m."

Karan waited with bated breath for her reply. Reena replied after a pause,"Actually I am waiting for my new friend Aditi, whom I met at the university, to come from Anand Niketan. If she agrees, I may come. Please give me your phone number I will inform you in about an hour."

Karan gave her the required number and after the usual pleasantries, he hung up. Karan felt grateful that Vivek was seriously trying to help him even during his working hours.

In the mean time, while sitting there waiting for Reena's reply Savita inquired about Reena further. Karan frankly told her whatever he knew about her. Vivek started making jokes in between and the three had a good time laughing together.

After about half an hour the telephone started ringing, Savita picked it upand when she found that it was Reena, she gave it to Karan, who said, "Hi Reena! It's Karan. What's your program?"

"Well, I talked to my friend. We will come to the exhibition. My brother also insists on coming so the three of us will come directly to Pragati Maidan. My friend knows the place. Tell me the time and exact place to meet."

Karan fixed the time and entrance gate number where they would meet. He looked at his watch; there was sufficient time at their disposal. Karan asked his friend if he wanted to go to his office for some time, but Vivek said, "Our meeting was preplanned, so I kept myself free."

Karan breathed a sigh of relief, thanking his friend for all the trouble hewas taking for him.

Karan, Vivek, and Savita reached Pragati Maidan fifteen minutes before the time fixed with Reena. Karan bought six tickets and they waited near the entrance gate. After a few minutes, he saw Reena getting out of her car along with her brother and friend. Karan went toward her and said, "Hello Reena."

Reena soberly responded and introduced her brother and friend, "Karan, meet my brother Sumit and my friend Aditi." Karan shook hands with them saying, "Hello Sumit, hello Aditi, how are both of you?"

Reena's driver Basheer Khan drove off to park the car. Vivek and Savita joined the group and were introduced. They all entered the Pragati Maidan. Vivek was careful not to say anything to Reena, as her brother and friend were present. Neither spoke about it being a pre-planned program, Reena told her brother, "He stays at Nath's farmhouse opposite ours. We met at Sagars at the birthday party. Papa also met him once and he knows his family well."

It was the start of September and the end of the rainy season. This year, August had received plenty of rain. Only a few days ago there had been continuous rain for six hours. The weather now was dry and only mildly warm. Special cabs, open on three sides were running free of cost to carry people from one end of Pragati Maidan to the other. They got into a cab and reached the other end. From the way they talked, Karan could sense that Sumit and Reena were amazed to see such a beautiful exhibition ground in India, which was compared well in cleanliness and vastness with the exhibition grounds of other countries. They entered one of the big halls. All the halls were air-conditioned, and the latest technological innovations were on display. There was a lot of hustle and bustle and excitement.

Sumit was taking extra interest in exploring the different products. Karan asked Vivek to help him understand some of the items. They took about forty-five minutes in the first hall. There were concrete roads duly marked with paint and lined with trimmed flower trees. The halls were between grassy plots and flowerbeds on both sides of the roads. There was a large artificial lake with small fountains; the water of the lake appeared blue. Music was played in unison with the water flowing from the fountains. There was a big restaurant on one side of the lake to cater to the visitors. The scenery was eye-catching. The exhibition was a composite one. Both the industrial as well as domestic products were on display.

Several times Karan and Reena moved off together, either ahead or behind the others by a few steps. As they were entering the fourth hall, and the others were ahead of them, Karan took the liberty of asking Reena to fixa date and time to meet. Instead of replying, she just smiled.

When they left the fourth hall, they had been at the exhibition for more than two hours. Karan suggested having a cold drink at the restaurant and they went inside. They choose a corner table near a window so that they could enjoy the view. After Karan gave the order for the drinks and some snacks, he asked Sumit, "Did you like the exhibition?"

"Fantastic!" was the short reply. From his expression, one could easily guess that he liked whatever he saw at Pragati Maidan very much. They started talking about the different things that were displayed. Then their talk centered on other visitors who were in colorful dresses. The latest trends in fashions were discussed. Reena praised the well-managed and well-organized Pragati Maidan. Sumit asked Karan, "*Bhaiya*, how long do these exhibitions last?"

Karan replied, "Small exhibitions run for three to four days whereas the larger one runs for a week or two. There are exhibitions throughout the year with short gaps in between."

"Is that so? Then I would like to come here every month. Will you accompany me *bhaiya*?"

Karan was delighted, but looked at Sumit quite normally and said, "Why not? All these exhibitions are specific except a few like the present one, so in case the topic interests you, just ask me and we can come here."

"What do you mean by specific?"

"A specific exhibition means it is only for books and stationary or only for interior decoration and furniture or handlooms and handicrafts or automobiles and their accessories and so on."

"I see!"

The drinks and snacks were served and enjoyed by the group. Karan observed that Savita *bhabhi* and Reena got on quite well. Vivek was talking about general things. When they got up to

leave, both Vivek and Karan suggested that they see two more halls rather quickly so that they get out well in time. On which Sumit protested, "Why two halls and not all? Does it close so early?"

He looked towards Karan, who replied, "No it closes at 8 p.m. but for more time you have to ask your sister."

On which Reena smiled and spoke to her brother, "I promised mama we will be back at 7 p.m. positively. We can come again some other day."

Sumit did not object any longer. Karan observed that the two ladies were walking together and looked like old chums. Vivek and Karan talked softly, not about the exhibition, but about what was in their hearts. Karan also took care to see that most of the time either he or Vivek talked to Sumit.

After enjoying the other two halls, they came out near the gate from where they had entered. They went out to look for Reena's car and spotted her driver who brought the car from the parking area. Savita insisted Reena and the others drop by on the way home for a cup of coffee at Lajpat Nagar. To Karan's pleasant surprise, she agreed and said, "Savita *bhabhi* we will stay for a few minutes only."

Like Vivek and Karan, Reena and Aditi also started calling her *bhabhi*. Savita sat in Reena's car to show them the way. The two friends were now alone in Vivek's car. Vivek started making jokes, but before that, he told his friend quite clearly that he was impressed by Karan's choice.

They reached Lajpat Nagar within ten minutes. Savita served them snacks, coffee, and soft drinks. During their conversation, she took Aditi's telephone number, thinking it might be useful for Karan. Karan could not get an opportunity to talk directly to Reena.

While seeing them off Savita said to Reena, "Please do visit us when you geta chance and also ring me when you reach the farmhouse. I think my phone number is with you."

"Yes, I have it."

The three got into the car and Reena stuck her head out of the windowand said, "*Bhabhi* do come to our farmhouse sometime."

Karan sat with his friend for another twenty minutes. In the meantime, Reena called Savita to inform her that she had reached home after dropping her friend off on the way. Karan thanked both Vivek and Savita for their help in arranging such a fantastic program and then he took their leave to go to Ashok Vihar.

CHAPTER 10

Karan returned to the farmhouse early in the evening on Sunday, and after refreshing himself, came to the drawing room for evening tea. Both of the elders were there. Vinod was discussing some papers with Premnath. Karan wished his grandmother and granduncle and shook hands with Vinod as they finished the work and the tea was served. Karan and Vinod were meeting after a good gap so they inquired about each other. Premnath addressing Karan said, "How are your parents and everyone at Ashok Vihar?"

"They all remember you and Grandma and sent both of you good wishes."

Gayatri Devi, as if recollecting something said, "Yesterday when I talked to your mother in the evening you had not arrived there."

"Yes, Grandma yesterday when I was with my friend Vivek at Lajpat Nagar we made a sudden program with his sister-in-law, Savita, whom you know, to see the exhibition at Pragati Maidan. It all happened so suddenly, that I could not inform you or mother."

Premnath inquired, "What was the exhibition like?"

"It was really very good. All the arrangements were excellent. There were a variety of new products on display."

Once the tea session was over, Karan went with Vinod to his room. It was the second room along the corridor on the right of the entrance to the main farmhouse building and faced a large drawing-cum-dining hall. The first room on the right was the office, where Vinod was normally available during the day, carrying out his duties. The office had two cabins and two work desks with computers. Opposite Vinod's room near the other end of the corridor, there was the door to the servants' hall. Between the servants' hall and drawing-cum-dining hall there was a huge kitchen, which had three doors one of which opened into the hall, the other one to the servants' hall, and the third to the kitchen store. The servants' hall had attached toilets and its main entrance was from the backyard. On the other side of the hall, there were two sets of rooms opposite each other. The front one was occupied by Premnath and the other one opposite was occupied by Gayatri Devi. There was a corridor separating these sets of rooms. Two stair cases led out from the end of the hall opposite the entrance of the main building. The left staircase leads to the library just above Premnath and Gayatri's accommodations, and the other lead to four rooms, opposite each other with a corridor separating them. There was a balcony on all sides of the hall at the first-floor level.

Karan occupied the room just above the office facing the front of the farmhouse whereas Vinod's room was adjacent to the office room, also facing the front. All the rooms in the farmhouse had attached toilets and an attached balcony. After chatting for some time, with Karan laughing at Vinod's jokes he left with his stomach aching from excess laughter and went to his room.

When Karan came down stairs for dinner, he saw a couple sitting on the sofa chatting with his grandmother and granduncle. Karan noticed some resemblance between the men sitting on the sofa with Reena's father, but he was sure that this man was not her father. Karan said Namaste, and was introduced by Gayatri Devi, "Meet my grandson Karan, who is working in an MNC consulting company at Bhikaiji Cama Place." Then pointing toward the guests, she said, "Karan dear, Mr. and Mrs. Mukherji, our neighbors from the opposite farmhouse."

Karan gave a broad smile and sat down. In reply to the introduction, Mr. Mukherji said, "Well young gentleman, happy to meet you." On which Karan profusely thanked him.

Gayatri Devi looking towards her grandson said, "Their son is getting married, and they have come to invite us for the reception."

Karan saw a wedding card with a gift box placed on the central table, and he could see the link. Mukherji further extended the invitation by saying, "Both of you do come along with Karan. My family and my younger brother and his family who came here recently will be happy to meet you."

Premnath now took the lead and asked, "Have your younger brother and his family come here to settle down or just for a visit?"

"He has come here permanently, along with his family, after getting VRS from the I.F.S."

Karan was now sure that the couple sitting in front of him was Reena's uncle and aunt. The guests took their leave, and they all went outside the main building, where Mukherji's chauffeur-driven car was waiting. Both the families bade farewell to each other and after getting into the car, the Mukherjis' departed.

Premnath and the others went directly to the dining table. It was a big table with fourteen chairs. Karan asked his granduncle, "Where is Vinod?"

"He will eat his dinner in his room as he is busy with some bank paperwork which he has to get ready by tomorrow morning."

When they started dinner Gayatri Devi said, "Mukerji's younger brother and his wife met us last year at some parties."

At this Karan also felt he should disclose something and said, "I also met Mukherji's younger brother and his daughter by chance. We were introduced to one another as neighbors. His name is Subhash C. Mukherji, when he discovered that I am your grandson and Mr. Premnath is my granduncle, he started speaking very highly of both of you."

Both Premnath and Gayatri Devi said in unison, "We feel that he is a very nice and decent person."

During the week, Karan was quite busy at the office on a special assignment. He was closely associated with the project along with other officers and would return quite late, at 9 p.m. or even later. He ate dinner at the office as it was being provided there. While going to or coming from the office every day, he looked at the Mukherji's farmhouse gate with bated breath and high expectations that he might see Reena. Whereas he knew very well that at such hours, there was no possibility of her appearance at her gate. But who can stop a person in love from taking shelter in impossible possibilities? His manner of looking towards the Mukherji's farmhouse was so strong that it became an involuntary action, as Reena's face glowed with high luminous intensity in his heart.

It was Sunday at last! The project was completed by Saturday evening and handed over to the client. Karan got up early in the morning, came out to the lawns, and jogged a few rounds of the farmhouse. After about ten rounds, he sat down on the front central lawn. The weather was mild and a cool breeze was blowing. He asked Sheru to bring him a cup of tea. His mind was running quite fast. He heard the different bird sounds like musical notes and the heart of the lover started thinking about his next move so that he and his beloved could come together. He wondered if he could call her his beloved, and then he replied to himself, why not when he loved her? Here lay the problem – he did not know her heart. He only knew her outward expressions; or in his dreams where he could listen to her heart, as they sat face to face revealing the deep recesses of their hearts to each other. When he came back to reality a few minutes later, he started weighing different ideas with the help of which, a long meeting with Reena could take place.

CHAPTER 11

Mr. and Mrs. Subodh Mukherji visited Nath's farmhouse for the first time when they came to invite Premnath and his sister to their son's marriage. During the last few years, Subodh Mukherji had been very busy with his export business. On seeing Nath's farmhouse, both husband and wife were amazed at such artistic landscaping and the beautiful garden. Although Nath's fame as an architect and landscaping expert was well known, a business-minded person like Subodh Mukherji had no time for such things, even though they were neighbors for a few years. Subodh Mukherji shifted to the farmhouse about four years ago. Before that, he lived at Vasant Vihar, one of South Delhi's posh localities in a villa that was now used as his office. Two days before the marriage, the Mukherji brothers were sitting with their wives having tea. Reena was also present when her uncle and aunt started admiring Nath's Garden. Reena on overhearing this reminded her father that the gentleman he had met a few days ago near the bank lived in the same farmhouse. Her father recollected the gentleman as well as his association with Premnath and the grand old lady, Gayatri Devi. When the senior Mukherji couple went to their portion of the farmhouse Reena asked his father curiously, "Papa, may I go with mother someday to see Nath's Garden? You know how much I am interested in gardening. Moreover, both uncle and aunt were admiring it so much, that I have become quite curious."

"Sure dear, you can go."

The Mukherjis had arranged a grand party on the lawns of their farmhouse for their son's wedding reception. Premnath and Gayatri both decided to go and were keen that Karan accompany them. They spoke to Karan on the day of the party. His grandmother told Karan in the morning, "Dear Karan, don't forget tonight is the reception at the Mukherji's so do come home on time."

"Oh Grandma, is my going to the reception compulsory?" Karan asked casually when he wanted desperately to go so that he could get a glimpse of Reena.

"Why not dear? You have been directly invited by the host." "All right then I will try my best to come home on time."

After a few minutes, his granduncle came in where he was eating breakfast. Karan had breakfast early on working days, as he had to rush to his office. Karan wished Premnath who said, "Young man, do you remember that tonight there is a reception at Mukherji's farmhouse? Be here on time from your office."

"Yes Sir, I have promised grandma that I will come on time."

The reception was a grand show with colored lights on all the trees and shrubs. Temporary fountains, again with colored lights, were set up and were spraying the water very beautifully. The main building was in the center of the plot, with two entrance gates at the corners. Today the gate nearer M.G. Road was open. There was a carpet from the gate to the premises of the main function. Mukherji couples were receiving guests at the gate. Premnath, Gayatri Devi, and Karan were greeted first by the senior Mukherjis and then by the younger ones, who received Premnath and Gayatri with great enthusiasm. Karan, while shaking hands with Reena's father, tried to remind him that they had met earlier and Subhash Mukherji.

Recalling his daughter's remarks about Karan three days ago, said, "Yes, yes, my son. I met you a few days ago when my daughter Reena was with me. Welcome and enjoy the party."

"Thank you, Sir."

Karan, his granduncle, and his grandmother went to the tables, where many guests were already sitting around. He saw Sumit,

Reena's brother who was enjoying himself with the youngsters, so he did not disturb him. He noticed that it was a gathering of mainly Bengali and Punjabi families. It seemed that care had been taken to spray the place, as there were no mosquitoes around. The weather was fine and light music was heard in the background. They chose a vacant table and sat around it. Waiters were moving around offering snacks, cold drinks, and fruit juices as well as wines and other alcoholic drinks. There were several counters with a variety of chaats and soft drinks, and for those who did not drink alcohol in the company of their families or were single; there was a bar of alcoholic drinks. Karan's eyes were in search of Reena. He took a fruit juice and continued his search.

Karan started drinking a little whisky or beer after starting his job. His father was also a light drinker and had told him earlier, "In case my son, you would like to drink, do have the first one with me." The father believed that there was no harm in moderate drinking, but if Karan drank, then the family should have known about it. So, Karan drank beer for the first time at a party where his father was present. Karan was a light drinker but never drank in the presence of his grandmother or granduncle.

Suddenly Reena came to their table, as if from nowhere, and addressed him, "Hello Karan! How are you?"

Karan became self-conscious as he found his grandmother and granduncle looking at the newcomer, but after a few seconds of nervousness, he controlled himself, responded to Reena, and introduced her to his elders.

"Grandma, meet Ms. Reena, daughter of Mr. Subhash Mukherji."

Reena wished both with due respect and sat down with them. Looking towards Mr. Nath she said, "My uncle and aunt were praising the magnificent garden you have developed at your farmhouse. I am eager to see it."

"Oh! Good gracious, you are most welcome my child, come any time, any day. It will be my pleasure to show you, our garden."

Reena gave a broad smile. Gayatri Devi said affectionately, "My dear, when will you visit us? Do come soon."

"Well, I may come on Saturday with my mom if the day suits you."

"Every day suits us as we are both at the farmhouse on all days of the week. If Saturday suits you more it will be fine, particularly as Karan is also off on Saturday," and Gayatri Devi finalized Reena's visit for Saturday.

Reena offered them more cold drinks and snacks. Then she took their permission to attend to her other guests and left. Karan was full of thanks to God and his grandmother and granduncle for making Reena's visit to their farmhouse a reality. After dinner and wishing the newly wed couple, they said goodbye to the Mukherji families and returned home.

Saturday arrived at last, and Karan was expecting Reena. Karan normally did not miss going to Ashok Vihar unless he had work or some other pressing assignments. That day he had planned to go in the evening if Reena came in the morning; otherwise, he would go on Sunday and come to the office directly from there on Monday. He thought he was not going to miss the opportunity of meeting her under any circumstance. He went to the library after breakfast and chose a place to sit so that he could see anyone coming in from the gate. He picked up a book to read, but it was of no use. He walked up and down the library, but there were no signs of Reena. He picked up a magazine, thinking that he could skim through it without much concentration. But Reena did not turn up. By the evening he was feeling miserable and was sitting on the lawn with several magazines lying in front of him. He was just turning the pages without any interest. His grandmother came out, looked at him, and asked, "Dear Karan, what has happened? You look so serious!"

Karan smiled and said, "Grandma I am fine. I was just enjoying nature."

Karan's reply did not satisfy her. She asked again, "Do you have any problem with your job? Are you dissatisfied with your company?"

"On the contrary, Grandma I am quite happy with my job and the company. In this company, we have scope to think and work creatively and take decisions ourselves which is rare in other companies."

Gayatri was relieved and said, "I am very happy to know that you are enjoying your job."

Karan felt refreshed after talking to his grandmother because there was a break from the thoughts that were going round and round in his mind. He went to his bedroom and started reading Thomas Hardy's Tess of the d'Urbervilles.

He went down for dinner and found his granduncle, grandmother, and Vinod taking their seats at the dining table. His granduncle was talking about a special flower blossoming at that time. Karan listened attentively to Premnath then said, "Sir Nature is very accommodating. We have colorful flowers for all seasons. We are so abundantly enriched by nature, but we don't appreciate it enough."

"That's very true my son. We like to run after mirages and ignore what we have."

Karan came back to his bedroom after walking two rounds of the farmhouse with Vinod. He got absorbed in the novel he was reading. It was after midnight when he switched off the light and fell into a sound sleep, thanks to the book he was reading.

On Sunday Karan got ready and had breakfast with his grandmother and granduncle. He then went to the front lawn and sat on a chair under a tree. The heat was declining, since it was the end of September. Karan was enjoying the comparatively cool weather, but his mind was on Reena.

Neither had she come nor had she sent a message. Just then he saw Reena at the front gate with her mother. He got up quickly and headed towards the gate to receive them. They met each other midway. Karan greeted both the ladies.

They responded and then Reena said, "Yesterday we had to go to Apollo Hospital suddenly to see a relative who was admitted to the ICU."

Karan now received the answer to his questions, "How is your relative now?" he asked.

"Better. He received medical attention in time."

Karan showed both the ladies to the drawing room and requested them to sit while he looked for his grandmother and granduncle. He found his grandmother and brought her to meet the ladies. Karan knew that his granduncle would be in his laboratory. He spoke to him on the intercom and informed him about the guests. Premnath was there within minutes. Tea was served and Reena explained again why they could not come the day before and could not inform them, since they were preoccupied with the immediate family members of the patient. Premnath made the usual inquiries about the health of the patient and then requested them to come outside so that he could show them the garden. All of them went out to enjoy with the master, the beauty he had created out of nature, in his own style.

It took them about one hour to look around. They returned to the central lawn and sat down under the shade of a beautiful tree. Reena said, "Sir it's all so fantastic. I never thought that nature could be moulded in such a beautiful way while keeping its naturalness intact." Reena's mother, Rakhi, also praised the glory of the garden. Just as the serving boy brought some orange juice as directed earlier by Gayatri, Reena said, "Sir, I wonder if I can have a few lessons from you on gardening? I have always liked gardening and it is a favorite hobby of mine."

"Why not dear? You are most welcome. Come any time, for whatever little knowledge I have, I shall try to impart to you."

"Now you are joking Sir, it's not a little knowledge that you have; it's huge knowledge that you have acquired with the experience of years of experimenting intelligently with nature's beauty."

Gayatri Devi said, "Dear whether you come to learn gardening or otherwise, you are so sweet that we will relish your company. Do bring your mother also."

Rakhi Mukherji also invited them to their farmhouse and both the ladies prepared to leave. Gayatri asked Karan to see them off to the front gate, which Karan happily accepted. Karan returned and found both his grandmother and granduncle talking with each other. He heard them appreciating the good nature and decent manners of mother and daughter. Their appreciation was like music to Karan's ears. After listening to more of that for a few minutes Karan informed his grandmother that he would be going to Ashok Vihar in the afternoon and would go directly to the office from there on Monday. He went to his room and felt completely content at the outcome of Reena's visit. He simply could not ask for more. He was certain that Reena would come for gardening lessons regularly. This very thought gave him great satisfaction.

On Sunday night, he tried his best to pacify his mother regarding his marriage. Karan stressed that he needed some more time before deciding.

CHAPTER 12

Karan reached his office on Monday well in time. His company was also doing consultancy in market research and the Market Research Division was under Karan's boss Mr. Juneja. The manager in charge, Mr. Madhusudan who reported to Mr. Juneja came in with a problem when Karan was sitting in his boss's cabin. An NGO that received large funds from some socially conscious industrialists had offered a socially relevant market research project. The project had to be completed in a very short period.

Madhusudan's problem was that the officer under him was on leave because he had gotten married recently. He pleaded with Mr. Juneja to get the help of an officer from some other division under him to complete the work on time.

Juneja looked at Karan with some assurance in his eyes, as he knew Karan was capable of handling such a project. He asked Karan, "Will you help Madhusudan if you are not overburdened?"

"You can order me Sir, but the fact is that I would really like to do such projects as it's a subject close to my heart. I would like to do it irrespective of my workload."

"Good! From now you also work with Madhusudan on his project."

The basic purpose of the project was to find out from government records the money spent per year in a particular area on development and the actual development work done there. A number of parameters had to be followed. There were four districts in the area of study. After discussing the matter with Madhusudan, Karan drew out plans to collect the data from the four districts. He selected, with Madhusudan's help, the people who would collect the data, taking care of all possibilities to ensure that errors entering it were minimal. The schedule was prepared during the first two days and the teams went out to the four districts from Wednesday to collect all the data within about 10 days so that they would reach the office with the records and proofs well within a stipulated time. From the very next day, the data was first sent to Karan, who got busy preparing the initial reports basedon whatever information he received. He also consulted research papers, and books and had discussions with Madhusudan so that his mind was completely occupied till Friday. He felt relieved by the weekend that the progress was very satisfactory.

Karan reached the farmhouse late on Friday evening at around eight o'clock. He went straight to his room to bathe and came downstairs a little earlier than dinner time. All that week he came home late often having his dinner at the office, but he was expecting Reena to call him or tell his grandmother about her plans to take gardening lessons from his granduncle. After dinner, he sat in his room with the Thomas Hardy novel in front of him. He had read about sixty percent of it during the previous week and he was fascinated with one statement on love in the book: "No one falls in love; one is only raised in love."

He read until 1 a.m. and went to bed, but as soon as he was in bed Reena's face appeared in his mind and he again started dreaming about the time when they could both explore each other's hearts.

The next morning, when Karan went down for breakfast, Gayatri Devi was already around. The housemaid, Shobha, was arranging the breakfast.

Premnath also came in from his laboratory. After the initial pleasantries, they ate their breakfast and sat down on the sofas. Karan asked them to wait for a few minutes and went to his room. He returned with two parcels of woolen garments.

He gave one each to his grandmother and granduncle, explaining, "My colleague brought these from Ludhiana; they are a specialty of the city."

Karan regularly gave them gifts since he started working. The day he shifted to the farmhouse, he made it a routine to bring them expensive gifts on some pretext every month. He knew he could not offer to pay for his stay because that would offend them. Both kept objecting to the unnecessary bother he was taking. Karan simply smiled and said, "Both of you have given me gifts from my childhood and I always accepted them so happily. Now that I am a grownup earning person, accept my small offeringshappily."

Suddenly, as if recollecting something, Gayatri looked at her watch and said to her brother, "Reena should be coming any moment."

She then called the housemaid and gave her the parcels, telling her to put them inside the room. Karan heard the words about Reena, and he wanted to hear them again and again. Gayatri continued, "She will be coming with her maid. I asked her to have lunch and evening tea with us."

Karan was busy assessing the sweetness of his grandmother's words. He was speculating on whether the honey was mixed with the words or whether it was in his grandmother's mouth. He heard them without a single word or change of expression. His entire attention was on the sweet conversation between the elders. After a few minutes, he came out to the front lawns, dropping the idea of going to the library as he had earlier planned.

CHAPTER 13

On Sunday Karan reached Ashok Vihar in the morning and after spending some time with his parents, left for the club meeting, which was to be held nearby, telling his mother that he would return in the evening.

Karan reached Rohan's house well in time. All founder members and the seven others who became members later were present. At these meetings, members used to present socially relevant papers and make announcements about those members who had done something significant to follow the clubcharter, which was rewarded with applause. Karan, after reading the book which he had bought on India, liked a number of the topics discussed there in that he wanted to share the same with the other members of the club. His turn to speak came after lunch.

He came to the speaker's desk and started speaking, "Dear friends I have just read a wonderful book on India and its contributions to the world. We normally know about one or two out of these. Whereas there are several contributions, but presently I want to tell you about at least four such contributions, which changed and benefited the world enormously. The concept of God that was floated in India more than three thousand years ago is like the concept of Nature propounded by modern scientific philosophers. Modern scientific philosophers based their theories on a long spell of scientific research and technological developments. Strangely enough almost similar definitions were conceptualized by Indian Rishis based on spiritual, creative imagination plus the scientific development that had taken place until that time in India."

He continued, "The second major contribution is the concept of zero (*Sunya*) One cannot imagine any mathematical advancements or technological developments without the great concept of zero. The computer language, which is based on the binary system, is nothing but zero and one. The zero was also discovered more than three thousand years ago.

There is another major invention in the field of mathematics. The third contribution is the invention of the decimal system. Can anyone imagine any progress in mathematics or the physical sciences, which has resulted in all the technological development without knowing about zero and the decimal system? The next concept is the theory of karma which gets strength from the findings that genes pre-determine our lifestyle. The theory of karma was conceptualized as part of the Indian philosophical system more than four thousand years ago. It was linked to the theory of reincarnation. Both concepts are also accepted as part of the Hindu religion. The concept of reincarnation is also used these days as a psychotherapeutic technique called regression-based therapy. Today, the concept that reincarnation and rebirth are based on the theory of karma is accepted by a few Western philosophers and the literary people of repute."

Everyone was listening in pin-drop silence. Karan further continued, "The Germans picked up the thread and became well versed in Indology. They became the torch bearers of scientific developments in the nineteenth century and were responsible for the high level of technological advancements in Europe."

Before closing his presentation Karan said, "My purpose for presenting these facts is to develop a feeling of self-worth and be proud of being an Indian."

There were two more speakers after Karan, and after that, the official program was over. Karan met his friends and tried to update himself about them. Neither he nor Vivek said anything about Reena when they came across each other.

On Monday, Karan was again very busy with the social research project. A lot of data that had been received and compiled was updated with the new material brought in by the teams working in the field. Karan and Madhusudan were busy reading and finding the meaning behind the compiled data. This process continued until Thursday. Madhusudan was of all praise for Karan. He did not hesitate to appreciate him in the presence of his boss, Mr, Juneja, and said, "Due to the model developed by Karan, the data were collected very fast and compiled simultaneously at our office here."

The results were ready on Friday itself, three days ahead of schedule. On Friday evening Karan was sitting in the boardroom of his office along with Mr. Juneja and Madhusudan who were presenting the results of the project to the executive director and managing director of the company. It was a very important document that was to be presented to eminent people involved in the country's affairs and the management did not want to take any risks.

According to the results of the research, a lot of money was misused in the name of development. Ninety percent of the money spent was nowhere to be seen. Only ten percent of the funds were spent, whereas to keep the system going on, at least twenty percent of the funds needed to be spent. Thus, there was an actual deterioration of the system instead of developing it. During the discussion in the boardroom, everyone there was of the view that the same situation was prevalent throughout the country. That was the reason why, with the passage of time, the system had deteriorated instead of progressing. Karan could feel the anger and revulsion towards those public servants and politicians who were laundering, public money for their own use and putting the country in a situation that was worsening with time. Karan also felt a revulsion against those unethical businessmen who were looting the public with both hands. He seriously felt that more public awareness resulting in mass movements was required to make a change in the present dismal scenario. After dinner, which was served in the office, Karan returned to the farmhouse quite late and with a heavy heart.

CHAPTER 14

Reena's admission to the M.A. course was confirmed in late August and the session started in the fourth week of August. Initially, she went to the university in a chauffeur-driven car, then accompanied by her assistant-cum-maid, Luxmi, she started driving herself. She made many friends, all girls, in the very first week of joining, but she was closest to Aditi, who lived in Anand Niketan, a posh South Delhi colony. Both the friends visited each other on the weekends. The farmhouse where Reena lived was a double-storied building. She wanted to make her garden as beautiful as Nath's; not out of any competition feeling, but because she loved nature and had a taste for gardening. Throughout her life, she lived in big houses with gardens. She felt a fascination for flowers and greenery and gardening became her hobby. Reena's uncle Subodh Mukherji also wanted to convert his garden and make it as attractive as Nath's from the day he saw it, but in his case, it was more because of a feeling of competition. He even tried to get detailed information from Reena and on her suggestion; hired an additional gardener who was a qualified person. They already had two gardeners and they were told to take instructions from Reena only and to work under her guidance. From day one, Reena's ability to grasp Nath's gardening and landscaping ideas were quick. She started implementing whatever she learned from the master.

She came on the next Saturday at the specified time along with Luxmi, who went to the staff hall.

Reena and Gayatri met as if they knew each other for a long time. Reena and Karan went out with Premnath. Premnath explained the different varieties of trees in front as well as at the rear of the building for two hours. It was so fascinating that none of them realized the time until Sheru brought out glasses with a jug of juice. Karan while sipping juice said, "Sir, I never realized that every tree has such a long history of development and how you with your innovative techniques, were able to transplant them from different geographical areas to grow into such beautiful trees."

Reena simply said, "It is fantastic!"

Premnath suggested, "I think we may start a detailed study about gardening from next Saturday." Karan and Reena kept silent, agreeing to Premnath's suggestion. Karan got a sudden thought and said to Reena, "Granduncle conceptualized a public park just three or four kilometers from here, on a forty-acre plot at the request of the Municipal Corporation of South Delhi, which was then developed accordingly."

"Is that so? I would like to see a park conceptualized by him. Why don't we make a program together with our families, preferably next weekend?"

On overhearing this Premnath suggested, "All right. Both of you make the program and tell me accordingly, I may like to explain a bit to both of you about the concept behind developing the park when we are there."

They came back into the hall. Reena after calling her maid took permission to leave and as usual, Karan went up to the main gate to see them off. He reminded her, "Reena, please make the program to visit the park with the families next Saturday which is also a public holiday. I think it will be a very satisfying experience for you."

"Yes, I will speak to my mother."

They bade farewell and Reena disappeared. Karan again due to Luxmi's presence could not get a single minute alone with her. He told his grandmother that he would like to go to Ashok Vihar after lunch.

On Sunday when Karan returned home after meeting one of his school friends and was ready to sit down for lunch with his parents and sister, his mother called out, "There is a phone call from your friend." It was Vivek. Although they met at their club meeting last week they could not talk about Reena. That's why the first question Vivek asked was, "What progress have you made with Reena."

Karan gave Vivek the details of the past few weeks at which he said, "At least now meeting her is no more a problem and you are the best judge about choosing the time when you can express yourself."

"Yes. When is your marriage?"

"I think it will be in the first or second week of December."

On Wednesday, Reena spoke to her mother about visiting the park. Rakhi spoke to her husband, and he replied, "I have no objection to the program."

"Then you also ask dada (elder brother) and *bhabhi* if they would like to come with us."

"If both sister and brother are coming then the program will be really interesting, but I think dada and *bhabhi* can't go as they are going to Kolkata tomorrow."

"*Bhabhi* never told me about going to Kolkata."

He explained that the development took place that day itself. As dada had to leave urgently to Kolkata for business, he told *bhabhi* on the phone. She requested him to book her tickets also. There was a marriage in her family, but she had decided not to go as she did not want to travel all that way alone. Subhodh Mukherji and his wife turned up while they were talking. Rakhi immediately

asked, "*Didi* (sister), are you going to Kolkata tomorrow."

"Yes, we have decided it quite suddenly. I have come to ask you if you need anything from there or if you want to send anything to your family."

Rakhi thanked her sister-in-law and made out a small list of specialties from Kolkata she wanted her sister-in-law to bring back. In the meantime, the brothers were busy discussing some business matter in a low tone.

Reena's parents decided that they would visit the park along with the Naths and Rakhi informed Gayatri Devi on the phone. Both the ladies decided to take a homemade lunch with them so they agreed on the items each one would bring.

On Saturday morning, the car from Mukherji's farmhouse followed the one from Nath's. Subhash Mukherji was driving, and Rakhi was sitting in front, while Reena, Sumit, and Luxmi were at the back. In Nath's car, Karan was driving with Premnath sitting in front and Gayatri, Shobha and Sheru at the back. They reached the park gate within ten minutes where the name of the park 'Swadeshi' was engraved. Karan bought the entrance tickets, which was a nominal amount, and both the cars went inside.

Karan helped the maids and Sheru take the lunch boxes, mats, etc., to a grassy enclosure of small plants edged with a row of flowers. The mats were spread out under some trees, and everyone sat down. Another mat was spread for the food, disposable plates, and glasses, which were kept under the care of Sheru. The park was developed on a magnificent scale with lots of landscaped greenery, beautiful flowers, and trees. After the initial pleasantries, Reena was the first to speak to Premnath, "Sir how did you get involved in the park project?

Premnath first gave a smile and then said that it happened just by chance. On Reena's repeated request he narrated the incident: "One day I went to Delhi Government Office to meet an IAS officer regarding certain facilities for our farmhouses on behalf of the Farmhouses Association along with two other office bearers.

While we were discussing the matter with the officer, by chance someone made a reference to my two books on gardening and landscaping. On hearing this, the IAS officer took special interest and asked me if I would associate myself with the proposed park which was to come up near our area. I told the officer that I have no objections but with the condition and I will be doing it without any remuneration. He became so interested that he came with his team within the next two days to get the agreement finalized and signed. When I signed the agreement, he told me that his son was a student of architecture. He had heard of me and had read both of my books. He also told me that he took the file for approval himself so that the matter could be speed up. He was the Area Development Director of South Delhi and seeing genuine interest in a government officer, I was glad I have decided to get associated as a consultant to this park project."

There was satisfaction on everyone's face. Gayatri Devi and Karan knew of the details, but Karan took the liberty to comment, "It's rare that a government official takes a genuine interest."

Soft drinks were served, and they moved further into the park. Sheru was asked to look after the material they brought.

Reena and her parents had seen several beautiful parks in different countries. It was natural for them to compare them with this one. The park was crowded with families and individuals wandering around. It was completely landscaped and sectioned into different backgrounds. After roaming for about half an hour and seeing a small part of the park, which had a pond and a small bridge, Subhash Mukherji said, "It is really a new concept. Whatever we have seen in other developed countries is not as wonderful as this one."

Rakhi agreed with her husband, but she expressed it differently, "After having a look at your garden I guessed this park would be a good one, but it is far better than what I had expected. It seems as if I have seen a mini-Taj Mahal before and now I am looking at the real thing."

Premnath only said, "Well Mrs. Mukherji, your daughter has been praising my work excessively all these days, but you have even crossed her."

Everyone laughed at that. They sat at a grassy site for a few minutes, then Premnath led them to the other side of the park where there were a few natural waterfalls. Premnath informed them that the falling water was reused with the help of pumps, which were not visible. Pumps took water from the pond to the extent that it remained at the same level in the pond and pumped it to the height of the artificial hills. The entire scene looked like a natural one. Had he not told them that the water was reused, they would never have thought it was man-made.

They entered a valley of flowers. One could see flowers of numerous varieties. It was so pleasing to the eyes that one could sit there for hours and hours. Premnath told them another strange fact. "Some behavior therapists bring their patients along with their family members here to develop creative imagination in their patients. In the presence of these beautiful flowers, their neurosis gets reduced over time. When they are asked to imagine this valley of flowers which they have seen while sitting here with their families, they do it very easily resulting in the problem being cured."

After strolling around and enjoying the sights for about three hours, they returned to where they had started. They sat down and lunch was served, which they enjoyed while cracking jokes and talking of interesting anecdotes in their lives. Karan's eyes met Reena's on a number of occasions but they could not talk to one another whereas their eyes were saying a lot of things to each other. He was not yet prepared to express his love for her. He felt that there was still time to wait and watch. After a few minutes of rest, they got up to explore the unseen areas of the park.

They came to concrete pathways lined with roses of different colors and equidistant trees. Sumit was asking Premnath questions, which he was answering patiently, explaining things in detail. Sumit expressed great satisfaction after getting replies to his queries. The scene changed again.

There were fountains in line with blue tanks in round-shaped covered places to sit. The area was made of granite flooring in matching colors. There were a few architectural structures made of colored stones, from which they could not take their eyes away.

With such a sweet memory, they came back to their farmhouses quite refreshed.

That night when Reena was in bed, she started seeing again in her mind, the things she had seen at the park. Then her thoughts turned to the people living in Nath's farmhouse. There was a feeling of enthusiasm about them. Everyone looked lively, whether she thought of Gayatri Devi, Premnath, or Karan. She happened to meet Vinod Sharma when last time she was there, and he too seemed lively. As she extended her observations, she realized that even the gardeners, watchmen, and other domestic help all had that underlying enthusiasm, which develops in a system full of lively ambiance. She could feel that things were managed differently at Nath's farmhouse because of the outlook of the people living and working there. She wanted to create the same environment in her farmhouse. A smile came to her face and with a new determination, she went to sleep.

CHAPTER 15

Karan received a hospital-based project. The administration of a private hospital group wanted to increase the efficiency of the hospital without increasing any risk factors for its patients. The hospital chain was a reputed one, but in comparison to some other hospitals, its productivity and efficiency were on the lower side. In short, the operations performed per surgeon per day were quite lower than the competitive hospitals.

Karan identified the basic problem and worked on the solution. He got books on time and motion study, on increased productivity and efficiency from his office, and library and was busy studying in the office as well as at home. He visited the hospitals with two assistants and visited other hospitals to observe and note down certain points.

His office provided him with a staff of four people at his disposal to help in collecting data. He was asked to complete the project within three weeks. Complete involvement in the project helped him to keep his mind off Reena.

On Saturday morning, Reena came with her maid to the front lawns where Premnath, Gayatri Devi, Karan, and Vinod Sharma were sitting together having a discussion. Luxmi went to the staff hall to meet her friend Shobha, who met her halfway and took her to the hall meant for the staff. The staff hall was a reasonably big room with a dining table and six chairs. There were also four easy chairs with a small table out of which two were then occupied by Luxmi and Shobha. Sheru was asked to take drinking water to the front lawns and Champa to bring water for them. Luxmi did not see any staff hall for employees at Mukherji's farmhouse. It looked very pleasant to her to see that the staff could sit in a hall and had a place to sit or eat comfortably and honorably. After a few minutes, Rajaram and Revati came in from the kitchen and were pleased to see Luxmi whom they had met earlier. Revathi said to Luxmi, "Now that breakfast is over. May I make something for you?"

Luxmi replied, "No thanks, I have already eaten a heavy breakfast," and the four of them indulged in a routine talk.

Premnath took Reena and Karan to show them the laboratory and Vinod Sharma went to his office for his routine activities. Karan had already seen the laboratory a few times, but for Reena, it was a very different experience. Premnath was conducting experiments on a variety of plants. The laboratory had two rooms on the first floor above the garages whereas there was a balcony in front of the Lab in the office which was also on the ground floor. All the rooms were air-conditioned. Behind it was the six staff flats. On one side of the office there were two garages and on the other side was fiberglass shed, where experimental plantations were carried out at the specified temperatures. From the stairs inside the office, they all went upstairs and entered the laboratory through the balcony. Numbers of instruments were lying on a granite slab. There was a table with a few chairs and a computer. Both rooms had the same arrangement. Premnath explained the instruments which were being used there to find better qualities of seeds and plants for breeding and crossbreeding and growing plants on the stems of other plants, etc. They went to the fiber glass shed where Premnath showed them the plants growing in the controlled environment. Then they returned to the office where after looking closely Reena was quite impressed with the landscaped drawings that Premnath was preparing on the computer. While this was going on, a watchman came to inform him that Mr. Varma was waiting for him in his car outside the gate. On hearing Varma's name Premnath suddenly recollected and said, "Oh! I forgot that there was a Farmhouse Association meeting today for which Mr. Varma has come to fetch me."

Premnath immediately stood up saying he was sorry for interrupting the training process, "All right, dears, we will meet the next weekend." Karan and Reena also stood up and Reena said, "Surely Sir, I will be coming on Saturday."

While going out, Premnath asked Karan to tell Gayatri Devi that he would be coming for lunch at about half past two.

Reena and Karan went into the house and told Gayatri Devi, "Grandma, granduncle has gone for an association meeting. He will be coming to lunch at about 2.30 p.m."

"So that's the reason both of you have come back from the class so early!"

She called Sheru and asked him to bring some tea. The weather was mild, so tea was a natural choice. Reena was looking towards the side table on which a few books were lying. She asked, "Karan, are you reading these books?"

Karan smiled and Gayatri Devi replied, "Both Karan and Premnath are good readers whereas I read occasionally, Vinod also is a good reader."

Karan said, "Granduncle has a large library with a number of books on a lot of subjects."

Reena inquired with curiosity, "Where is the library?"

Gayatri suggested immediately, "Karan, show Reena the library after drinking your tea."

"All right Grandma," replied Karan, and addressing Reena he added, "I will also show you granduncle's beautiful book collection."

He spoke intentionally, to have more time with Reena alone.

They got up and Gayatri Devi said, "I will call you both when Premnath comes for lunch. Is that all right Reena?"

"I am already giving you a lot of trouble Grandma, please don't insist on lunch."

"You are a strange girl, calling me a grandma and talking about giving trouble in the same breath."

"Sorry, I will have lunch with you."

"Now you are on the right track."

With a smile on her face, Reena accompanied Karan to the library upstairs. She liked the atmosphere of the library. The books had been cataloged by Vinod. They sat near the window that opened to the front of the farmhouse. Reena looking toward Karan said, "One must be enjoying a lot while sitting and reading here."

"I mostly sit here when I read. I sometimes read in my room which is also upstairs and the front view from there is similar to this one."

They kept silent for a few minutes. Karan thought it was an appropriate opportunity to open his heart. He looked at her and found her looking at him. He attempted to collect his courage and said, "Reena, earlier I wanted to tell you something but could not dare. Today I feel I should talk with you about the matter which has been troubling my mind for the last few months."

He tried to see the reaction on her face, but finding no substantial change, he continued, "Reena, I first saw you at the bookshop, even before the birthday party. Perhaps you did not notice me, but at that very moment, I felt a strange attraction towards you. Some call it love at first sight."

He stopped again, but still seeing no reaction, he continued, "I don't know how you will feel about all this, but the fact is that I am in love with you. My heart is filled with love. I even think I am becoming a better person because of this feeling of love. I am anxious to know how you feel about me. At the same time, I won't ask you to reply now. Please take your own time and tell me at your convenience."

Both kept silent for the next few moments. Karan then said, "If you like, we can go down now."

Reena came alive suddenly and said, "Well, it's time to go now."

Gayatri saw them and said, "I told you that I will call you when Premnath comes."

Reena said, "Grandma, I have some urgent work so I may not be able to wait for granduncle. Next time I promise you that I will have lunch with you."

Gayatri, seeing Reena's face permitted her to go. Reena sent a message to Luxmi who came immediately and after saying goodbye, she left. Karan kept standing with his grandmother at the doorsteps of the hall looking at Reena.

Premnath came about half an hour after Reena left. They ate lunch and Karan went to his parents.

In bed that night, Karan was trying to analyze Reena's possible reaction to what he had said that day to the girl he loved. His desperation was obvious, but being a rational creature, he wanted to give her sufficient time to discover her own feelings. He well understood the practical angle, that there was a lot of difference in their financial status. He was hopeful about Reena's parents on this count as they were well educated and would not give much credence to what he owned. Presently he wanted to concentrate on one point only and that was her feelings towards him. Was there any similarity between her feelings toward him and his toward her? Thinking about this he succumbed to sleep.

That same night Reena lay awake in bed. Sleep was nowhere in sight. She wanted to understand her feelings, but it was not an easy exercise. An attempt to know one's exact feelings toward someone for the first time was really a difficult one, particularly for girls of Indian descent. From the day she met Karan at the birthday party, she considered him, a good friend. No doubt, she sometimes wanted to meet or talk to him. In fact, she had not gone further than thinking of him as a good friend whom she liked to meet. Her friend, Aditi, who accompanied her to Pragati Maidan, spoke highly about him. She picked up the thread from the day she first met him and started thinking about all the incidents during their meetings. She realized now that Karan was attracted to her from the start, but the things that now appeared apparent were not earlier so. Reena was also assessing the point when love was expressed by one person to another. The whole picture was very unclear in her mind. She changed track a bit and started thinking of her reply to him at their next meeting. She could sleep only after two hours in bed.

On Sunday morning when she got up, Karan's face flashed in her mind. Earlier also Karan would come to her mind, but never the first thing in the morning and the last thing at night. After bed tea, she came outside and was involved in the garden instructing the gardeners. With an extra effort, she tried to come out of Karan's spell.

Her parents were present at the breakfast table. Reena ate without a word, which looked a bit strange to her parents. Her father asked her, "Reena; what's the matter, my dear? You look unwell. What happened? Are your gardening lessons at Nath's running well?"

Reena was not expecting such a question at that juncture from her father.

As she was absorbed in her thoughts she spoke abruptly, "Papa I am all right. My training is going very well and I am really enjoying it."

Her reply satisfied her parents.

Reena could not enjoy college on Monday. Aditi, her best friend, observing a change in her repeated the same question a number of times, "What's the matter, Reena? You seem to be off mood."

Reena's reply was the same, "I am quite fine and normal. Why are you asking again and again?"

During his working hours that week, Karan remained busy with the hospital project even up to 8 p.m daily. He thought about Reena before going to sleep but on Friday, sleep was nowhere to be seen as he was tense about her reaction. He even wondered if she would come.

On Saturday Karan got up and got ready quickly, ate breakfast in a normal manner, and went outside to the front lawns. He thought he would not ask or try to get a reply about her feelings today. If she wanted to tell him on her own accord, it would be good, otherwise, he would ask her only after giving her some more time.

Reena came with her maid and Karan was at least free from one tension; the uncertainty about her coming. Both naturally wished each other.

Premnath gave his lesson as usual. He was happy to impart knowledge to eager young minds and he had no inkling if something else was going on in their thoughts. Gayatri also had no inkling about it. Reena's parents took her friendship with Karan as a very normal development between neighbors. Her parents even took their earlier meeting at Pragati Maidan very casually. While taking the gardening lessons, both behaved normally. As per her promise, Reena even ate lunch with them. Their eyes met a number of times but no communication was possible due to the presence of Premnath or Gayatri Devi or both. After lunch, Reena went back with her maid and Karan left for his parents. While leaving, he told his grandmother, "I may go to my friend Vivek on the way."

Karan thought it right to tell Vivek of the developments on the Reena front as he kept calling to inquire.

On Monday he reached the farmhouse a bit earlier than the routine time of the previous week. There was sufficient time for dinner, so he went to Vinod's room. Vinod was working on the computer in the office. Karan asked, "Are you busy?"

"No, no I am just doing routine work which can be done at any other time."

After saying this, he switched off the computer and took Karan to his room. Karan inquired, "How is life?"

"Things are pretty good here. Tell me about yourself. Is there any special adventure?"

Before Karan could speak Vinod said, "Sorry before you tell me, would you like some whisky?"

"Well, I take beer normally, but now that it's November I will take a small peg."

Vinod took two glasses and a bottle of whisky from the cupboard along with a packet of chips. He served the whisky and they toasted each other.

Karan said, "I want some advice from you."

"Oh, you are self-sufficient in this regard but if I can be any way useful to you I am always available for any kind of service."

Karan tried to collect some courage and then said, "I am in love."

"Is that so? Who is the lucky girl to whom our Karan has given his heart?"

"She lives opposite our farmhouse. She is Reena."

"She is Reena! She is really a nice, beautiful girl. I have met her." Vinod continued, "Please tell me more about it, when did all this start?"

Karan said, "I am going to tell you when it started, and I also want your views on my further course of action."

Vinod kept quiet and Karan told his love story from the very first day he had seen her to the time when he expressed his love to her.

After listening to Karan, Vinod said, "It's all wonderful; you are doing very well till now."

Karan put his puzzle, "Now should I ask her for a reply or let her tell me at her convenience?"

Vinod thought for a few minutes then replied, "Well that depends. Some people are so desperate that they want a reply at the moment they express love. At least in your case, you have given her time to think about all the pros and cons. It's a good gesture. I think you can ask her next time when you meet her as she has had enough time to think about it."

Karan found Vinod's reasoning, quite logical. The clock struck 9 p.m. and they went down. Gayatri Devi and Premnath were already at the dining table.

CHAPTER 16

Vinod sent a message to Shobha through the intercom to send his breakfast to his room. Premnath came to his room at the same time. Even though he was Vinod's boss and could call him anywhere at any time that he needed to, he had no problems coming to Vinod. He learned of this system of getting work done by subordinates when he was in the USA. In India, the bosses gave themselves too much self-importance. Vinod wished Premnath, who responded and said, "Vinod, I am thinking of writing my next book."

"That's very good Sir, what can I do to help you?"

"You can do a lot. I know how much help I got from you when I wrote my last book." He then handed him the list and said again, "I need the books mentioned in this list. A few will be available in the market; the rest you willhave to get from the British and American Libraries."

"All right Sir, I will go in about half an hour."

Premnath's library membership cards were in Vinod's custody. He took the list and said, "Sir, first of all, I shall try the libraries. If I don't get them there, I will search for them in the market."

In the meantime, Sheru brought Vinod's breakfast.

"That's fine. Please carry on with your breakfast," and Premnath left the room.

It was Vinod's practice to inform Gayatri Devi whenever he went out of the farmhouse. It was not necessary, but Vinod felt that if some work needed to be done, he could do it. Before leaving Vinod said to Gayatri Devi, "Grandma, I am going to Connaught Place to get some books for Sir. Do you need anything?"

"Yes, I need a few household items from the Green Park Market. I willgive you the list. Take Sheru with you."

Vinod left the farmhouse in the staff car with Sheru. It was the normal practice that whenever Vinod had to buy household items, someone was sent along to help, as the quantities would have been usually quite large. Gayatri Devi insisted he calls her grandma. Earlier, he called her Madam, but she objected saying that Premnath might be his boss, but she was not.

Gayatri Devi was happy at the moment, as last week her daughter, Sulakshana, called to say that she would be coming to Delhi in the third week of December. Sulakshana, her only daughter, lived in Jalandhar about 350 kilometers north of Delhi. It is natural the world over that mother-daughter ties are unique, and particularly in India, where family ties matter so much, their relevance is felt even more. Whenever Sulakshana came to the farmhouse to stay, Gayatri Devi and Premnath celebrated the occasion by throwing one or two parties. She was also thinking along those lines that day.

Her two sons who lived in Ashok Vihar visited her at least once a month. This year, however, they did not come as often, since Mudra, was appearing for the twelfth-class examinations, which were crucial for her future career. Gayatri was now thinking of calling all her children and grandchildren to the farmhouse during the Christmas vacations. Mudra would stop her coaching classes from mid of December to concentrate on studying for the examinations to be held in March, so during the Christmas vacations, when schools were closed and no coaching classes were on, she thought, was the best period for her sons and their families to visit her. Mudra could study at the farmhouse. While she was visualizing the possible future events, Champa came to tell her that their driver Sohan Lal's daughter had a temperature of 102°F, since the morning. She called Sohan Lal immediately and was first angry that he did not tell her earlier. She then called the family doctor who arrived within fifteen minutes and attended to the girl. Gayatri again told the staff, "Whenever anyone is not well I must be told immediately." Gayatri took a lot of interest in the education and health of the children of the staff and Premnath always praised her for her noble work.

Karan's schedule at work was as hectic as the previous week since the project on enhancing the productivity and efficiency of the hospital chain was still in progress. The work was carried out at the sites as well as in theoffice and Karan was supervising both places. He was to submit the report by the next week.

After waiting for six clear days, which felt no less than six long months, Saturday came along with Reena and Luxmi. She entered the drawing-room, where Karan was sitting with his grandmother. Gayatri Devi met Reena affectionately with a close embrace and asked Champa to bring some juice even when Reena objected. Luxmi went to the staff hall as usual. Karan told Reena that his granduncle was in the laboratory so both had decided to go there.

When they entered Premnath's office, they saw him dictating to a lady who was typing on the computer. On seeing them, he said, "Please come in."

Reena said, "I think you are busy Sir, are we not disturbing you?"

"Not really, but I want to complete this dictation, which will take about an hour. In the meantime, go and see the garden I will meet you near the green benches."

"All right, Sir," replied Karan and they left the room.

They went to the rear of the building near the pond and on reaching Lover's Point Karan said, "Let's sit here for some time."

Flowers were giving off a beautiful fragrance and they could see one side of the pond from where they were sitting. Reena said, "This whole place around the pond is fabulous. I would also like to develop something very similar if granduncle would give me some lessons in landscaping."

Karan was just watching her while she spoke. Then their eyes met, and Reenastopped speaking, blushed, and smiled. Karan thought that it was an indication to change the topic, so he mustered his courage and said, "Reena have you thought about what I said to you two weeks ago? May I know, what is your response?"

He paused for a few seconds and then continued, "I want to clarify one thing, if your answer is no, we can continue as good friends. Feel free to give an honest answer, without fear."

Reena kept silent for two minutes, which seemed to Karan like an endless period, and said, "If the answer can be in one word then I say…yes."

"I can't believe my ears! Today you have given me a priceless gift."

They were silent for some time, and then Reena said, "Frankly I took our relationship to be that of neighborly friendship, but after you spoke, I was forced to think about the whole affair from a different perspective and got peace of mind only when I got my reply."

"Reena you are fantastic! I always wanted a girl like you. I have not told anyone, not even my mother or grandmother who keeps asking me whether I have selected the girl of my choice."

"So now you can tell them."

"No, not now, first you talk to your parents. If they agree, then I will tell my mother and grandmother who can then talk to your parents."

"Why?" Reena asked smiling. Karan replied, also smilingly, "What is the result of mutual love between two young hearts?

As if you don't know. It's the marriage of two minds, bodies and souls. Is it not so?"

Both laughed. Reena looked at her watch. An hour had already passed so she said anxiously, "Let's go to the green benches. Where are they?"

Karan led her to the place where there were two green benches opposite each other so that people could sit face to face and talk. Reena said, "I should not tell my parents immediately. Let me have my classes for another two weeks. If I tell them now it may be difficult for me to come here."

Karan thought it over and said, "You are right, but when will you tell your parents?"

"I will tell them during the Christmas holidays when we go to Kolkata for my cousin's marriage."

Karan found no fault in her choice of timing and replied, "Well, as you think best."

He was about to speak again when he saw his granduncle coming towards them. Premnath explained the finer points of gardening, showing them flowers or plants as examples for two hours. When he finished Reena expressed her desire, "Sir, I want you to teach me about landscaping also. I would like to learn during the next two to three Saturdays before the Christmas holidays."

"Are you going somewhere during Christmas? That period is the best time to learn about both gardening and landscaping, as the weather is suitable, and you will be free from going to the university."

"I would love to learn during that time, but I am going to Kolkata for my cousin's marriage."

"I see, then from our next session, I shall try to explain some basics of landscaping. You will be busy with your studies after coming back from Kolkata."

"Yes Sir, I shall start again only after my university examinations are over."

They returned to the hall and Gayatri, as if ordering Reena, said, "Today my dear, you will not go without lunch."

"I would like to stay, but mother told me that she is preparing a special fish dish for me, so I will have to go."

"Then I won't insist. Being a Bengali, any fish preparation is a special dish."

All of them smiled, Luxmi was called, and Reena departed.

When they were alone, Karan said, "Sir you were quite busy dictating something to your assistant."

"Oh yes. I have started writing a new book."

"That's very good news, accept our good wishes," both said in unison.Then Gayatri said, "That's why Vinod went out to get some books. It's really good that you make regular attempts to fulfill your creative endeavors."

On this Premnath said, "The credit goes to you, as you have made this place a heaven for me and I always have extra energy to perform more and more."

"Thank God, if I am in any way useful in fulfilling your creative endeavors."

Karan was smiling at hearing these affectionate words between the sister and brother.

Karan could not sleep that night. He was quite satisfied with the development. At the dining table, when his mother asked the same old question he replied, "Mother dear, I intend to marry at the end of next year so there is plenty of time to finalize a girl."

"All right, at least you have specified a time limit today."

His father was listening to the conversation between the mother and son. His reaction was a simple smile, without any objection.

Karan and Reena were both invited to Vivek's marriage, which was fixed for the first week of December. Karan was planning to introduce Reena to his club friends.

During the next week, he was busy completing the hospital project report. On Wednesday morning, two days earlier than scheduled he was sitting with his boss, Mr. Juneja, with the complete project report and explaining the results. "Surgeons should not waste their time in hospital administration or other pre or post-operation activities. Any such activities should be looked after by trained staff or doctors other than Surgeons. The administration of the hospital needs to be looked after by an Administrator. These recommendations will result in everyone performing their jobs in an optimum way, with less fatigue. This in turn will result in more operations being performed within the same time frame, which means more efficiency without inviting extra risk. Mr. Juneja agreed with Karan's conclusions and the project report was handed over to the client.

While reading books on time and motion studies for the hospital project, a thought flashed through Karan's mind about what Shri Krishna said in the Bhagavad Gita about performing one's duties in the best possible way (resulting in higher productivity) without bothering about the results. He felt as if there is a link between the conclusions of time and motion studies and that of Gita. The only difference that seemed to him was that "the Gita is a superior document, as it treats the human being as individuals and not machines, taking care of their consciousness."

CHAPTER 17

Karan reached the farmhouse well in time. While enjoying tea with his elders, he said to his granduncle, "Sir, I hope your book writing is going well. Can I be of any use to you in this endeavor?"

"Certainly, you will be very useful! I have some data which I want to analyze based on certain parameters and your experience at consultancy can help me."

"Sure Sir, you can call me at any time."

Karan then turned to both the elders and said, "My friend Vivek's marriage reception is on the day after tomorrow and he has invited both of you for the function. He has also invited my parents. Will you like to attend the function?"

Premnath and Gayatri Devi looked at each other's faces, then Gayatri said, "You will be in the company of your young friends. It will be better if you enjoy yourself with them, but you must call the newly- wed couple to the farmhouse one day. We would like to congratulate them."

Gayatri Devi and Premnath had already met Vivek a few times. They found him a very decent and amiable person. Karan informed his parents about the invitation and their reply was the same as that of his grandmother.

Reena also spoke to her mother about Vivek's marriage reception. Savita, Vivek's sister-in-law also requested Reena's mother on the telephone to accompany her daughter to attend the reception party. Reena made the program of attending the marriage function along with her maid and her friend Aditi who was also invited. Reena's brother Sumit couldn't go, as his examinations were to start on coming Monday.

On Thursday, Reena called Karan at the office and informed him that she would attend Vivek's marriage reception. They fixed the time when they would start from the farmhouse. He came out at the fixed time and within two minutes; Reena's car came out on the road. When Karan came near her car, she waved to him from the backseat of her car which her driver Bashir Khan was driving who knew Karan well and it was also in his knowledge that both the neighbor families were friendly. Karan always spoke well to all the working-class people. So his politeness and consideration of such class had made him popular with them. Whenever Karan passed the Mukherji farmhouse, the security staff always used to salute him. His popularity with the Nath farmhouse staff was also well known.

The reception was held at the Hyatt Regency, located on Ring Road. They first went to Anand Niketan to pick up Aditi. Vivek's marriage was held in Chandigarh two days ago at a simple ceremony, which was attended by a few family members only. Vivek wanted Karan to come to Chandigarh, but Karan excused himself. Vivek's father forced Vivek to agree to a large reception at a five-star hotel because he had to invite all his business contacts, but the marriage at Chandigarh remained a simple affair without any dowry. Thus, Vivek fulfilled one of his commitments to the club charter. He compelled his father not to accept any gifts or money from the guests. His father was a rich man with a strong business instinct. All his life he had given gifts to others in their marriages, but here to fulfill his son's lofty ideals he suppressed his business instinct. So he not only agreed but also got it printed very clearly on the invitation cards.

On reaching the hotel, Bashir Khan dropped them at the entrance to the hall and went to park the car. The names 'Vivek and Kaveri' were displayed in golden letters on the board near the entrance.

Reena, Aditi, and Luxmi stepped inside the illuminated corridor where they were received by Savita, who introduced them to her husband, Abhishek, as her new friends. Karan, who was a few yards behind them, as he had to park his bike, was greeted by

Savita and Abhishek. As Reena heard Karan's name she stopped and waited for Karan to reach her. Karan touched Vivek's parent's feet as they were standing for the reception to receive the guests and he then accompanied Reena's group to the main party premises. Luxmi got permission from Reena to move independently and to join them later.

The hall was large enough to accommodate more than five hundred people. It was fully carpeted and brightly lit by chandeliers. There were two beautifully carved large chairs placed on a stage for the newly-wed couple, who had not arrived yet. They selected a table and sat down.

Waiters were moving between the tables continuously with different snacks and drinks. Karan, Reena, and Aditi were looking around, making comments, and chatting. For Karan, Reena's company was the biggest attraction and for Reena, it was Karan's company. The newly- wed couple entered, surrounded by a group of girls from both sides. There were cameras and flashlights in front of them, with cameramen inching backward with every forward step made by the couple. Finally, they sat down on the chairs laid out on the stage. The three of them decided to wait before going up to meet Vivek and Kaveri as many people started coming forward to congratulate them. Karan was also searching for his friends. He got a glimpse of Sujeet Singh at some distance and went there to meet him and met his other friends Puneet and Rohan chatting with Sujeet Singh and his wife. Karan paid his respects to Sujeet's wife, Simran, but when he couldn't see Puneet's wife he asked him, "Where is our *bhabhi*?"

"She is in an advanced stage of pregnancy."

Karan knew that Puneet's wife was pregnant but did not know that she was not able to come. Puneet's friends had already made him give a party, when they heard, he was going to become a father. Karan changed his mind about introducing Reena as the girl he loved. Instead, he decided to introduce both Reena and Aditi as Savita bhabhi's friends and Reena as his neighbor. He requested them to come to the other side as he had a few companions there. He led them to the table where Reena and Aditi were sitting and introduced his friends and Simran, clarifying that Reena was his neighbor and they had contacts at a family level. Simran, Reena, and Aditi got together and started enjoying the party. Karan felt it was time to meet the newly-wed couple. They all got up and moved towards the stage. On seeing them coming, Vivek said something to Kaveri. Vivek got up to receive his friends but was forced to sit down again. When Reena was introduced to Kaveri as Karan's and Savita's friend, she responded as if she knew her very well. Photographers there took their photographs in different positions and after a good degree of bonhomie, they returned to their table after chatting for ten minutes.

Light music could be heard in the background. There was a dance floor with a DJ and at the request of the gathering, popular dance numbers were being played. Young boys and girls started dancing. It is a normal tradition in India that on such occasions, close relatives of the newly-wed couple dance and have a good time. It is an expression of their happiness. Karan could see Savita dancing with Abhishek. The atmosphere was electrifying with music, dance, and laughter, coupled with people chatting. This continued for an hour. Then a few people started moving towards the tables where dinner was laid out. Savita and Abhishek came to their table and requested them to have dinner. Abhishek went to attend to other guests but Savita found time to sit with Reena and the others for a few minutes, chatting with them. When Abhishek came and insisted on taking dinner, they got up. As soon as they stood up, Karan asked Abhishek, "May I check, if Reena's driver has had his dinner?"

"They are all taken care of. There is a separate arrangement for them near the parking area with a super-hit musical film show."

"That's a good gesture."

Halfway to the dinner tables, Savita and Abhishek took leave to take care of the newly-wed couple. It is customary on such occasions that the family members from the boy's side invite the guests from the girl's side to dine together only after attending to the other guests. The arrangements were simply fabulous. They enjoyed the dinner and came back to sit at a table which was available. Sujeet wanted to say goodbye, but Simran was not willing to leave. Moreover, she had the excuse that Vivek and his family were busy having dinner at that time. Their party had split into two groups from the start, one of the four men and another of the three ladies. Slowly, Rohan, Puneet, and Sujeet got some information about Reena and Karan's affair. Actually, they had got a hint last week when Savita and Abhishek met Sujeet and Simran by chance in Karol Bagh market where they were out shopping and they decided to have lunch together. The inkling that something was up was strengthened during this function. When Vivek's family finished dinner they all got up to take their friend's permission to depart. After the final pleasantries, they came out of the hall and Luxmi joined them midway. After getting promises from Reena and Aditi that they would soon be visiting her, Simran allowed the group to separate. Karan said to Reena, "Let me ask Bashir Khan to bring the car while you wait here."

Karan came back within two minutes and told them that Bashir would be bringing the car. Aditi could not resist herself and said, "Karan *bhaiya*, your friends are fantastic. I really appreciate their good manners and Simran is so sweet."

"It gives me great pleasure on knowing that you feel so good about my friends."

Reena also aired her views. She said, "I fully agree with Aditi." "That is even better."

In the meantime, Bashir brought the car. Karan said something to him and went to get his motorbike. When Karan came with his bike, Bashir started the car. Karan's bike followed Reena's car. Aditi was dropped at her house at Anand Niketan and the car proceeded to its destination.

Within the next half an hour, Karan was in his bed but there were no signs of sleep. He was thinking about his friends' comments about Reena, which they expressed in low tones. Their tone was low, but their comments were very high. There was a smile on Karan's face as he recollected all that was said about her.

CHAPTER-18

As soon as Reena was in bed she started thinking about Karan. When Karan conveyed his feelings toward her, she also started to think about him. She was amazed and could not believe that she had started liking Karan so much. A number of times, she became eager to tell her mother about her affair with Karan, but she managed her feelings every time because she was quite certain that going to Nath's would be almost restricted. The proper time, she knew, was during the Christmas holidays.

Earlier it was Karan, who kept on waiting for Saturdays, now Reena had the same eagerness. It was rather a strange phenomenon that Saturdays became shorter, and the waiting days became longer. On this Saturday the situation for Reena was different. It was not just a short day for her; it was her last day to take a lesson in gardening and landscaping from the master. The Christmas holidays would start next Saturday and their flight to Kolkata was on the same day in the morning hours. During the lesson, Premnath observed, "You seem a bit serious today."

She forced a smile and said, "Sir next week I am going to my maternal grandparents in Kolkata. There I will also attend my cousin's marriage so it is going to be a double attraction for me."

"Then why do you look so gloomy? Well, there may be some misjudgment?"

Reena did not reply and gave another forced smile. Karan's

position was not in any way better. He remained a listener to the conversation and conscious that his feelings would be detected and wanted to avoid the same. After the lesson was over, Premnath spoke to them, "Now the first stage of the course is over. You have taken an immense interest with plenty of questions and picked up the knowledge very well. Both of you proved to be my valuable students." He said laughingly.

Karan and Reena thanked him for giving up his precious time. Karan said,"You know granduncle is writing his third book these days."

"It is great news, but I feel quite guilty for taking up his precious time."

"Why do you feel guilty? I enjoy talking about gardening and landscaping. I can talk about it for hours together each and every day."

When they came to the main building, Reena spoke to Gayatri and tried to get her permission to return home immediately. Gayatri reluctantly allowed her to go without lunch. Karan went up to the gate to see her off. Both walked side by side with Luxmi a few feet behind them, but they did not speak as they were full of sadness due to the twenty days of separation.

Karan, due to his mood postponed going to his parents by a day and informed his mother on the phone that he would be coming on Sunday morning.

While eating lunch, Gayatri informed Premnath and Karan that she had received a telephone call from Jalandhar while they were busy in the garden. Premnath asked, "What is the news from Jalandhar?"

"Sulakshana is coming tomorrow evening."

"That's great news. Is she coming with her children?"

"No, she is coming alone. Both Piyush and Ria are going on college tours."

Karan said, "Then I will be meeting aunt Sulakshana on Monday, as I am going to Ashok Vihar tomorrow morning. I had promised to meet a few of my friends tomorrow afternoon."

Gayatri said, "I will explain it to Sulakshana. Your mother was telling me that Mudra's coaching classes are over and she will be studying on her own. I suggested that they can come here during the Christmas holidays. Mudra can bring her books."

On this Premnath reacted, "Your suggestion is wonderful. I expect plenty of hustle and bustle in the farmhouse!"

Premnath always gave a strong reaction and warm feelings whenever guests were invited to the farmhouse, particularly from Gayatri's family.

Gayatri's children also showed their affection for their maternal uncle and felt no inhibitions in visiting or staying at Nath's farmhouse for any length of time.

On Sunday morning, while Karan was sitting with his father, mother, and sister in the drawing room drinking tea, Karan's father inquired, "How is your job getting on?"

"Papa, earlier I would say that it is a good company and my job is satisfactory, now I would like to add that both my Company and my job are excellent."

He explained how he was getting the opportunity to work on different projects and how much the management respected his decisions. His father replied, "I am happy to know that you like your job and are doing well."

"Papa I am your son. I have learned a lot of things from you but the foremost is to do one's job sincerely and honestly. I always try to work to the best of my abilities and then never fret about the result."

His parents showed their happiness at this and Mudra who was listening with a smile on her face did not say anything. Karan changed the topic and spoke to her, "How are your preparations going on? I heard yesterday from my grandmother that your coaching classes are over."

"Yes, my course is over. Now I want to revise."

"Grandmother was telling me that you are coming to the farmhouse during the Christmas holidays."

The answer came from his mother who said, "Your grandmother is insisting as Sulakshana is coming. Mudra has to go to school until Friday so we may come on Friday evening."

"That's good news." Then looking at his watch, he said "Ma I have fixed an appointment with my friends. I will be returning late. Don't prepare lunch for me. I will have it with my friends."

"Well, then my dear son."

The friends had fixed this Sunday as the meeting day, at Vivek's marriage reception because Vivek would be back from his honeymoon by then. Other members were duly informed. The venue was again Rohan's apartment, which was ideal, and they held most of their meetings there ever since he rented the place. All the members came and lunch was ordered from a restaurant close by which provided packed meals. There were no special speakers on that occasion. It was an open discussion and started with civic amenities and went on to the rampant corruption prevailing all around. Most of the members were of the view that corruption became more rampant in Indian politics after Lal Bahadur Shashtri's demise. Karan was of the opinion that corruption was also a normal feature of life during the Mughal era, and the British, who was so maligned for their rule in India, actually succeeded in controlling that menace. During the last thirty years, corruption took strong roots again. Vivek concurred with the situation prevailing and said strongly, "We must pay bribes for every genuine work that needed government clearance for the smooth operation of our business. My father, knowing my beliefs, never asks me to perform such activities, but both my father and brother do as the Romans do."

On this Karan said, "Some people compare Indira Gandhi with Chanakya but I don't see any similarity between the two except that she was a strong leader. Actually, India needed a strong leader then, and I appreciate that quality in her, but alas! She was not as fair as expected."

The members seemed to be interested in what Karan was saying, so he continued, "You know how Chanakya's politics was aimed at the overall welfare of the country. He lived a very simple life, so how can we justify comparing these two historical personalities when only one or two qualities of Chanakya were present in Indira Gandhi!"

Sujeet Singh questioned Karan, "I have heard some great things about Chanakya but have not had time to read much. Have you read anything about him?"

"I read something really great about him recently whom very few people know but I think everybody should know."

"What is that?" Voices were called out from most of the people sitting there.

Karan said, "I will tell you. Chanakya trained Chandragupta Maurya from his adolescence with the aim of removing Dhananand, the ruthless ruler of Magadha, from the throne. Magadha, during that time, was the largest kingdom in India. Chandragupta, under Chanakya's guidance, not only defeated Dhananand and won Magadha but a few other kingdoms in India. He became the Samrat (king of kings) of almost all of India up to present-day Afghanistan. This was around 300 BC, I meant about 2,300 years ago. Chanakya became the prime minister and had total power. Chandragupta, being his protégé, did not do anything without his advice. At the height of his glory, Chanakya decided to pursue higher knowledge and wanted to relinquish the post of prime minister, but to competent hands. He also knew the king would not allow him to leave easily so he was trying to find a suitable person who would perform the duties of prime minister well. During that period when Chandragupta was the undisputed monarch of such a big kingdom, someone dared to attack the Maurya kingdom with a small force. He was defeated and captured. When he was presented to the royal court, Chanakya was amazed to see that he was Rakshasa, the prime minister of King Dhananand. When asked why he attacked the mighty Mauryas, he replied that he wanted to take revenge for his king. This reply stunned Chanakya. He was impressed by Rakshasa's faithfulness, who after such a gap of time still owed allegiance to his king. Chanakya was immediately struck with the thought that if he could succeed in changing Rakshasa's allegiance to Chandragupta, he was well experienced to take his place as prime minister. One could see how genuine Chanakya's purpose was, his daring thoughts and imagination. He tried to convince Chandragupta about his plan and at last the King very reluctantly agreed. Chanakya floated rumors about his differences with the King and Chanakya's men convinced Rakshasa that the rumors were true. Finally, the King offered the prime minister's post to Rakshasa. With a heavy heart, the king bowed to the wishes of his mentor. Rakshasa became the prime minister and Chanakya went to a hermitage in an isolated place with his wife to study and enhance his knowledge. The result was a great book written by Chanakya on the economic polity called *Arthashastra*. Chanakya was also known by two other names, Kautilya and Vishnugupt."

The faces of Karan's friends showed that they were really impressed by the character of the mighty Chanakya who gave up glory and power, found a competent man to replace him by floating a fake story, and went off to pursue higher knowledge.

Even Chanakya's all manipulations were for the good of the country only.

The friends were of the view that sincere politicians who worked for the love of the country are a rare species. Most of those at the helm of affairs belonging to different parties were simply a group of scoundrels.

They felt the need to awaken the people to this fact. Karan then proposed to start an NGO, which would work for national development and become the watchdog to expose corrupt politicians and public servants. It was emphasized that the work would not be easy as these corrupt politicians and public servants formed a strong lobby that tried to destroy anyone who came in their way and tried to obstruct them in their looting. In the evening when they bade goodbye to each other they decided to come prepared to form the NGO at the next meeting.

Karan could not sleep for a long time after he went to bed as he was thinking about the meeting and Reena. He felt that his emotional involvement with her brought to his mind a clearer vision and strength of purpose and created feelings full of inspiration. He remembered again Thomas Hardy's views expressed in his novel, about love. He smiled at the thought that real love was responsible for the individual's development to a higher plane and never to a lower one and went to sleep.

CHAPTER 19

Karan was quite absorbed in his work at the office on Monday morning when tea was served. He stopped his work for a few minutes to enjoy the tea. Suddenly he remembered that his aunt Sulakshana had arrived at the farmhouse. His mother had told him last night that she called them and had also inquired about him. He felt the urge to speak to his aunt, so he picked up the phone. When she came on the line he said, "Hello Aunty, how are you?"

"I am fine dear. How are you and when will you come home?"

"Aunty, I am very well and will be at the farmhouse before seven in the evening."

He asked about his cousins and uncle and chatted for about ten minutes before hanging up and returning to his work.

Karan's father was the eldest of Gayatri Devi's children and Sulakshana was the youngest. She was about forty-five years old, but like her mother, looked much younger. She could easily be called beautiful. Gayatri's two sons, Vijay and Ramesh, were simple in comparison to Sulakshana who liked pomp and show and was assertive by nature. She was married to an army officer, Rajdeep Khanna, who was a colonel and due to retire next year. Rajdeep's elder brother Pradeep retired as a brigadier the previous year. He settled in Jalandhar where both the brothers had built their bungalows on their ancestral land. Pradeep had two daughters; the elder was married and the younger one, Preity, was doing an MBA in Fashion Design from the Apeejay Institute at Jalandhar. Sulakshana was very anxious that Karan and Preity should form an alliance for marriage. She was beautiful and well-spoken. Sulakshana had little doubt that Preity would pierce Karan's heart with her beauty and talk. Preity and Karan were of course unaware of these plans. Priety had visited the farmhouse twice earlier with her aunt. Her first visit was as a school kid during summer vacation and Sulakshana had come with her own children Piyush and Ria. Preity had happy memories of the farmhouse and its inhabitants, but nothing particular about Karan. Her second visit was after her twelfth class examinations.

Karan was doing his graduation at that time and happened to meet her twice for short periods. Both the persons had shown little interest in each other. Sulakshana's children were now in college. Her son, Piyush, was doing engineering, and her daughter Ria was doing her first year in arts. Both of them have been regular visitors at the farmhouse during their school days, always coming to their maternal grandmother during their summer vacations. When Gayatri Devi was staying at Ashok Vihar, they went there first, and then together with their grandmother along with their mother and other cousins would go to stay at the farmhouse. Premnath was very happy on such occasions as he enjoyed the hustle and bustle of having his sister's grandchildren around.

Sulakshana, like her mother, enjoyed parties. Premnath on the other hand enjoyed giving parties but was always reluctant to attend others' parties. Only when Gayatri insisted and told him who the other guests were would he reluctantly accompany his sisters. The reason for that was in all the parties at his farmhouse, he was busy attending to his guests which he liked doing, whereas at other parties there was nothing for him to do and he was forced to listen to a lot of nonsense. Premnath was a person of high integrity and had no interest in wasting his time with superficial people discussing money, just to show off their wealth. It was customary for Premnath to organize a few parties whenever Sulakshana was around, as both mother and daughter ruled the party arena when together.

This time Sulakshana's stay was for two weeks, until the end of December. She spoke to her mother about a possible match between Karan and Preity who would be joining them next week. As Gayatri had no inkling about Karan and Reena's affair, she was genuinely interested to see if the boy and girl would like each other. When the four of them gathered for dinner, Karan asked his grandmother, "Where is Vinod?"

"He has gone to Ghaziabad for two days to attend his cousin's marriage."

Earlier Karan had been sitting with his aunt, talking about everyone in Jalandhar. He knew why Piyush and Ria could not come and also that Preity would be joining them next week. When they started dinner, Gayatri looking towards Karan said, "Sulakshana's birthday falls on the twenty-fourth of December. Premnath and I are planning to celebrate it by inviting a few close families. Your parents, sister and your uncle's family are coming. How many other families should we invite?"

Karan thought for a moment and replied, "It is an occasion worth celebrating. You could call two to three more families. As Vinod is not here please tell me if you want me to do anything."

"Vinod will be coming on Wednesday and the birthday falls on Friday so there is nothing urgent, but if there, I shall tell you. I think we can call the Mukherjis and Sagars.

Karan was happy inside but only said, "Reena told us they were going to Kolkata. If you want to call them it is better to check if they are here on Friday."

"I think Reena said they were leaving on Saturday, so they should be here.

Anyway, I will check before deciding about the others."

Gayatri Devi dialed Mukherji's number and spoke, "Am I speaking to Rakhi Mukherji or Reena *bitia*?"

"Namaskar *Dadima* (grandmother), Reena speaking," said Reena, recognizing Gayatri's voice. Gayatri continued, "Hello dear Reena, how are you? My daughter is here from Jalandhar. We are celebrating her birthday on Friday the twenty-fourth, and we would like to invite your family. Can you come with your parents?"

"Our flight is at about eleven in the morning on Saturday, so I think we should be able to come."

"If your mother is around, may I talk to her?" "Sure *Dadima*, I will call her."

Gayatri invited Reena's mother and the family. She also invited the senior Mukherjis and the Sagars. Then she called both her daughters-in-law asking them to come on Friday well in time for the birthday celebration. She also reminded them to bring their clothes for their stay at the farmhouse. Vijay promised his mother that he would take leave on Friday to bring his and Ramesh's family to the farmhouse well in time.

Vinod, who returned on Wednesday, arranged everything well in time. Karan also helped whenever needed. Gayatri was busy arranging the house with the help of her daughter. It was the first party at Nath's after Karan started living there.

On Friday morning, when Karan was going to the office everything in the farmhouse was as per routine except for discussions between Gayatri and Sulakshana. When he returned at about 5 p.m, he found the house full of hustle and bustle due to the presence of the guests. The three children, Mudra and his cousins, Vinnie and Ishu, were making the most of the noise. They were playing outside on the front lawns. On seeing him, they rushed to his bike and met him with great excitement. Karan responded with equal enthusiasm, and they all went inside. Karan touched the feet of his father, mother, and aunt Sunanda. Ramesh had not come yet. Karan sat for a few minutes with his father when Premnath joined them. Shobha arranged tea and snacks at the dining table where Karan, his father, and granduncle were sitting, and soon the ladies joined them.

Vijay Malhotra had an excuse for his brother, he informed, "Ramesh has a very busy schedule these days in the office due to pre-Christmas activities so he will come directly from the office."

Kamini and Sunanda were very happy to meet Sulakshana after a gap of about a year. They sat around inquiring about her family. Gayatri joined them after making a final round of the house to ensure that all preparations for the party were in order. The children and Premnath were together on the outer lawns. Premnath was answering their questions about the flowers and plants, and then leaving them to play; he went to the laboratory to complete the day's work. Sulakshana, while sitting with the other three ladies, found it the appropriate time to talk about Karan and Preity, particularly addressing Kamini was already eager to see her son as a bridegroom as soon as possible. She had no reservations about Sulakshana's proposition; on the contrary, she expressed her happiness if it worked out, as she knew Preity was a beautiful and decent girl, but, knowing her son, kamini expressed her apprehensions openly, "Karan will only marry the girl of his choice."

"Does he like someone?" Sulakshana inquired. Kamini replied, "He has not expressed his liking for any girl to me, but I don't know if he has someone in mind," and she looked towards her mother-in-law who said, "I also don't know if he likes anyone."

Sulakshana said, "I hope there is a possibility. As Preity is coming next week, I hope they will like each other."

It was Sulakshana's keen desire to see this proposition materialize because then she would be able to control two families, her in-laws as well as her parents. Her habit of controlling others was a feature of her personality. Many people try to control others to gain personal importance.

Reena came with her brother and parents. Her uncle's family could not come as her aunt was unwell. Sagar's family also could not come because they had to rush to Meerut as their close relative was hospitalized suddenly. Gayatri Devi introduced her family to Reena and her parents. Karan introduced the children from both sides. Reena's simple beauty and manners caught the attention of everyone there. The party looked like a beauty parade of young, middle-aged, and old. Without their realizing it, the gathering was full of beautiful ladies of all age groups each with different features. Kamini and Sunanda were the simpler ones.

The cake was cut by Sulakshana and everyone surrounded her and called out "Happy birthday". Gayatri put a piece of cake into Sulakshana's mouth and each person in the room did the same, except for Sumit.

Sulakshana regretted not bringing Preity with her. She was observing Reena and Karan and felt that Karan's eyes lit up in Reena's presence, but she was not sure. The party started getting lively and Reena noticed that her mother and Sulakshana got on well and sat side by side at dinner.

The children were served dinner earlier and when the elders were at the dining table, they were playing *Antakshari* (a game of songs). After the dinner was finished, they moved to the sofas, and coffee was served. The youngsters were disturbed by the elders sitting near them, so they went outside, where a canopy had been set up. Sumit whispered something to Reena, who announced that she was going outside with the younger ones and invited Karan to accompany them. Sulakshana noticed that Karan and Reena went outside and did not return even after fifteen minutes. She was curious and made a gesture that she was going to the bathroom, but went to the balcony of her mother's room. She looked out and saw Reena and Karan standing very close, talking to each other. She could also hear the laughter of the youngsters at a distance and guessed that they must be playing on the front lawns. She was now certain that something was cooking between Karan and Reena. Then abruptly she came back to the drawing room and joined the others who were busy talking. After about five minutes, Reena came in and Karan came ten minutes later. Nobody noticed these things except Sulakshana as she had already set her mind on a match between Karan and Preity, which she now felt, might be in jeopardy.

All the four rooms on the first floor were full on that night. Sulakshana occupied the room opposite Karan. Vijay Malhotra and Ramesh Malhotra's families were provided with the other two rooms. Sulakshana who was feeling a bit low after seeing Karan and Reena together tried to divert her mind by asking Mudra to share her room.

When Karan went to bed it was about 1 a.m. but there was no sign of sleep. Reena's presence, at the party and then so close to him in the garden, were the obvious reasons for that. It was a totally unexpected development that he was asked to accompany the youngsters and Reena to the garden.

When they came out Sumit asked Reena, "*Didi* will you both play with us?" Reena only looked toward Karan who replied, "I think Sumit dear you continue with your game of Antakshari, we would like to walk a bit."

The Nath farmhouse was well lit. Karan and Reena went for a walk towards the rear of the farmhouse. Reena assured Karan that she would talk about him to her mother in Kolkata. She also expressed her confidence that there was little to which her parents could object in their relationship. All this sounded very pleasant to Karan. While Reena was talking, she was very close to him. Until that day, he had never touched her but perhaps due to the imminent separation and sensual environment he felt the urge to embrace her, and the next moment, he did not know who had initiated it, but she was in his arms. They embraced closely; their faces were touching each other and their lips met. They separated and walked for a while longer without speaking until they came to the front lawns. Reena said, "Now I should go inside." And without waiting for a reply she joined the elderly group. Karan made a few more rounds of the garden and then conveying to the youngsters that he was going inside, he too joined them. Thinking about all this, sleep finally engulfed him and led him to sweet dreams.

In the Mukherji farmhouse, Reena was lying wide awake in her room. She started thinking about the sensations which she had felt just a few hours ago. She again got the same feelings as if something similar was happening. That scene was playing repeatedly in her mind like a film when she was unknowingly in the arms of the person to whom she started giving more importance than anyone else. That moment of embrace and the kisses thrilled her entire body. And the best part was, that she knew she did it because she loved him and believed him and did not feel guilty at all.

On Saturday morning Karan got up quite late. He felt the desire to go to the pond for some exercise. Within ten minutes, he was out at the rear of the farmhouse. The sun was out in the sky, but its effect was very pleasant, as it was the third week of December and winter had started. In winter, the Indian subcontinent changes into a golden period of sunlight. The days are pleasant and warm. Most Western tourists visit India in winter to enjoy the Indian sun and her beaches. Karan first did a few vigorous exercises, then he sat on the grass in a yogic pose to do some *pranayamas* (breathing yoga) and yoga. With a new energy level and a fresh mind, he started returning to the house, when the three children ran up to him. Karan greeted them and they responded with great excitement and requested him to take them to Swadeshi Park after breakfast. Karan agreed as he had no alternative. He also thought that in the company of the children he would get the opportunity to forget the pain of separation, which he was feeling intensely.

At the breakfast table, Karan asked his uncle if he would like to accompany them to the park which he reluctantly refused, as he had some work in his office, despite it being a Saturday and a holiday. Karan then asked Vinod who was sitting two seats away. Vinod looked at Premnath, who said, "Yes, Vinod can accompany you. He is free and the children will enjoy his company."

The children looked happier. Vinod was quite close to the Ashok Vihar families, which was why he was present at the breakfast table. Normally he had dinner only with the family. Karan, Vinod, Mudra, Vinnie, and Ishu went to the park, and Premnath, Gayatri, Vijay, Kamini, Sunanda, and Sulakshana came out to the front lawns to enjoy the winter sun and family talk. Ramesh was not there as he was urgently required at the office. Premnath also took his leave for two hours as he wanted to get a few pages of his book typed and his staff was waiting for him.

Karan, Vinod, and the youngsters returned from the park before lunch.

They were so happy that they kept telling their elders how much they enjoyed the beautiful park and the wonderful stories and jokes told by Karan and Vinod. Enjoying the family gathering, Premnath became emotional and could not resist saying to his sister, "I want the farmhouse full of people close to us who enjoy themselves and also make us enjoy their company." Gayatri Devi who understood the loneliness in Premnath spoke with equal emotions, "I always want to see you beaming with joy." Everyone sitting there enjoyed that outburst from the brother and sister.

The festive atmosphere at Nath's farmhouse remained until Sunday afternoon when Vijay and Ramesh were ready with their families to go back to Ashok Vihar. Premnath and Gayatri insisted that they stay for a few days more and that both brothers could go to their offices from the farmhouse. Again Mudra's examination preparations came in the way. She could not devote as much time as required to her studies while staying at the farmhouse. Sulakshana promised her sisters-in-law that she would be coming for at least one day to stay with them.

On Monday morning Karan was at the breakfast table when Sulakshana asked Karan, "Dear my niece Preity is coming from Jalandhar today. I will go by car with the driver to pick her up from the station. In the evening, I want to take her to the market at South Extension, as she wants to do some shopping. Can you come there in the evening to help us explore the market?"

"Oh Aunty, excuse me for today. I will be quite busy in the office and will come late in the evening." He again said, "I am really very sorry not to join you today evening."

"All right then please try to spare some time tomorrow." "Surely I will try Aunty." and he hurried to his motorbike.

CHAPTER 20

It was a very busy day for Karan in the office. When he reached the farmhouse, it was a quarter to nine. He saw a young girl sitting on the sofa talking to his granduncle, grandmother, and aunt. He guessed that she must be Preity. He went up to them and Sulakshana introduced them, "Preity he is Karan, my nephew, about whom I have spoken." Then pointing toward Preity, she said, "She is Preity, my husband's niece." Preity extended her hand, which Karan took and shook soberly, and sat on the sofa next to her.

Gayatri said to Karan, "Dinner is ready, do you want to freshen up?"

"I will join back within five minutes." He went upstairs and returned well within time. Vinod was also present. There was not much talk at the dinner table except about the food. After dinner, they came back to the sofa seats. Premnath started talking to the new guest. He inquired, "Are you a student?" She replied, "Sir, I am doing my MBA in fashion design."

"So now we have MBAs in fashion design also?"

Preity gave a smile in reply. Karan shared his views, "Nowadays there are many specializations. Advances in every field have resulted in this. It's happening in all professions like engineering, management, medicine, pure and social sciences, etc."

Premnath agreed with Karan, "So it seems. In our days there were few specializations, now there are many."

Sulakshana felt that the discussion was getting too serious on a topic in which she had no interest, so she changed it and said to Preity, "There are a number of movies running at the PVR if you are interested, we can all go to a movie tomorrow."

Gayatri said, "Better take Preity with you if you want to go to a movie. If Karan is free, he can accompany both of you."

That was exactly what Sulakshana wanted. She wanted Karan and Preity to spend more time with each other alone, except for her presence. She thought her presence would be a catalyst to further their relationship.

Premnath said to Preity. "Dear, you may go to the movie in the evening only. In the morning I promise to keep you busy by showing you some special varieties of flowers that were developed here by hybridization; you may not have seen them anywhere."

"Is that so?" Preity said with amazement and continued, "Then uncle, what are you doing here? Why are you not minting money with your findings?"

Premnath laughed and replied, "Dear, I have sufficient funds. Moreover, money is not everything. With God's grace, I have sufficient to live comfortably. Why should I yearn for more?

He laughed again, at which Preity showed even more amazement; she could not understand Premnath's philosophy. She was conditioned to think that more and more money would multiply one's happiness.

Karan was listening to the discussion and started thinking that there was no doubt about the fact that for poor person money and material possession was everything and until scarcity remained, they were undoubtedly the prime factors for happiness. He could not, however, understand why rich people with all kinds of amenities had the craze for more money and material possessions. He was sure these things were not responsible for furthering their happiness. He felt such persons who were having the wrong notion of more money or material possessions would not multiply their happiness.

Even in Bhagwat Gita, the only solution given to well-to-do people to further their happiness was to break their habits based on irrational thinking. His chain of thoughts was interrupted by his aunt who was offering him some fruit. He took a little and thanked her.

The next day Karan informed his aunt that he had arranged three tickets for PVR for the evening show and asked them to come there in the chauffeur-driven car at the specified time. Karan saw Sulakshana and Preity come out of the car at the PVR. Sulakshana waved to Karan, and he came towards them. Preity looked very smart and beautiful, and Sulakshana was simply gorgeous. All three went inside. Sulakshana arranged it so that Karan and Preity sat side by side. Her entire concentration was on the hope that the two would click. Karan and Preity started talking. During the interval, they went out to have coffee. Sulakshana observed them discussing different topics. It created a hope in her that something would materialize. They had dinner at a restaurant on the way back, as had already been decided. He gave Sohan Lal, the driver, some money to eat his dinner. The restaurant was full as it was very popular in the area. Karan tried to act as a good host during dinner. Sulakshana asked, "When are you coming back from the office tomorrow?"

"I will be quite busy because there is only one working day left this week."

"How is that?"

"Thursday and Friday are holidays for the new year, so there are four consecutive holidays."

She was happy to hear that Karan would be free for four days. She immediately chalked out a program and said, "All right then tomorrow I will go to Ashok Vihar to stay with my brothers for one day. I don't want to stay longer due to Mudra's studies."

"That seems a fine idea." Sulakshana's logic also appealed to Karan.

Sulakshana wanted Karan's parents to meet Preity, as it was necessary for her plan.

In the morning when Karan was eating his breakfast, his grandmother informed him that she was also going with Sulakshana and Preity to Ashok Vihar as his mother and aunt were insisting. Karan reacted to the information very positively, "That's great Grandma. It will be a good change for you. You can meet your neighbors and old acquaintances."

"I also think so. Will you come there from the office? Sulakshana was saying that your office will remain closed on Thursday and Friday."

"Perhaps that is not possible. Firstly, I will be quite late today and secondly, I have to go for a few hours on Thursday as there is an urgent client meeting. Moreover, I will keep granduncle's company."

"All right then."

Karan touched his grandmother's feet as she was going out for the day and went to his office.

He was busy studying a report when he got a message from his boss to come to his office. Juneja gave him a smile and said, "There is some good news for you. First, our client in Mumbai who heard of your reputation from someone has asked you to handle their next project. As the project is such that it can be undertaken only with regular coordination with the client you will have to go to Mumbai for about three to four weeks."

"Well, I can thank our client for the confidence he shows in me."

"The second news is more important and seems the outcome of the first."

He told him that the director intended to give him a promotion after his return from Mumbai. Karan immediately responded, "Sir it's due to your good comments about me."

"No, no Karan it's due to your performance that you will be getting a promotion."

He again thanked his boss and came out of his office with a face beaming with happiness.

Karan called his father during his lunch break and informed him about his visit to Mumbai and the promotion. He asked him to tell his mother. His father expressed a lot of satisfaction and blessed his son. Karan again became busy with his work. His phone started ringing and on picking up the phone he heard Reena's voice on the other side, "Hi Karan! How are you?

It's Reena speaking."

"Well, I recognize your voice. How are you? I am fine. I suppose you are calling from Kolkata. Have you talked to your mother? What is her reaction?"

"Yes, I am calling from Kolkata. I spoke to my mother about you. She likes you. Then she talked to my father. He also likes you."

"That's wonderful! Our problem is solved."

"Not completely. My father says he will talk to my uncle and only after his consent will he talk to your parents."

"Why is that? Can't your papa take the decision himself?"

"That's not the point. He is a very independent-minded person, but in family matters, he wants his brother to say yes before going ahead. He feels indebted to him. I will explain when I come back on Sunday. At present, my parents have agreed to

our relationship."

"That's fine. I hope your uncle will also agree. I have some good news too. I may be getting a promotion soon."

"That's wonderful! Accept my congratulations." "This is the

result of your entry into my life."

"Now you are kidding me." Reena said laughing and continued, "I got a cellular phone, a gift from my cousin."

"Oh, then I have to buy one also to talk to you more conveniently," Karan replied. Both wished each other a happy New Year and Reena disconnected the phone.

Karan was happy that he would be getting a promotion less than two years after joining the company. He knew he worked very hard both during the training as well as after that.

Karan reached the farmhouse at about half past eight. He found his granduncle busy with Vinod in the drawing room. He wished him and shook hands with Vinod. When he sat down Premnath said, "We were just waiting for you. I was thinking we may have a small drink session before dinner."

Karan hesitated and said, "Sir is it all right to drink with you?"

"Your father told me that you started drinking and your first drink was with him. I like your father's approach so there shouldn't be any problem if the invitation is from me."

"Well, Sir if you wish. It will be an honor to drink with you. I will just come in a few minutes."

"Vinod also showed the same reservation initially and I told him the same thing." Karan smiled and hurried to his room.

He joined them in ten minutes. Sheru placed the glasses, Black Label, soda, water, and snacks on the table. Karan poured the drinks and they toasted each other. Premnath was an occasional drinker, and this was the first time Karan was drinking with him as he himself had started just a few months earlier. Premnath started the conversation, "Today I am very happy as I completed a hundred pages of my book which is taking good shape."

"That's good news. Your writing speed is quite fast Sir." Karan said.

"Vinod's help in providing me inputs has speeded the progress," Premnath replied.

"Oh, Sir I did not do anything so worthwhile," Vinod said sheepishly.

Karan agreed with his granduncle and said, "Sir it is a fact that Vinod is making things easier for you. He is really quite capable."

Vinod took the matter into his hands, "Karan why do you forget that it is my job? I am supposed to perform it to the best of my abilities."

Looking at Vinod's discomfort, Karan changed the topic and asked his granduncle, "Where will you get it published Sir?"

"Well, my old foreign publishers are already in touch with me, but Vinod says this time we need to contact other publishers and we should go to whoever gives a better offer. He is looking for the details of other publishers on the Internet."

"Vinod's suggestion is really good." Then looking towards Vinod, Karan added enthusiastically, "Keep on dear."

He further said, "I also have good news from my office about a possible promotion in the near future."

Both congratulated him. Premnath said, "Why have you not informed us earlier? Our happiness would have multiplied."

"Actually, I was relishing your news about the book so much that I forgot."

They were late for dinner that day but enjoyed themselves. Karan went to bed quite late but again there was no sleep. Reena's face lit up in front of him and he was thoroughly enjoying it.

Karan went to his office on Thursday to attend the urgent meeting. After lunch in the office dining room, he returned to his room to hear the phone ringing. His aunt Sulakshana was on the other side. Recognizing her voice he said, "How are you,

Aunty? Are you speaking from Ashok Vihar or the farmhouse?"

"We are starting after some time from Ashok Vihar and will be at the farmhouse before six. When are you coming?"

"I will be there to welcome you." "That's good."

Yesterday when Sulakashana went to Ashok Vihar there was a lot of bonhomie among the sisters-in-law. Normally lunch was served late at Ashok Vihar as they had a late breakfast. Preity got very friendly with Mudra, Kamini, and Sunanda, but she tried not to disturb Mudra too much. She was busy watching her favorite serials before and after dinner. Sulakshana used that time to talk about Preity and Karan with Kamini and Sunanda in another room. She told Kamini, "*Bhabhi* at the first opportunity, speak to Karan about Preity. Only if he likes her will I talk to her parents."

"Preity is a beautiful girl, getting a good education and belongs to a good, known family. I also think it will be a good match." Gayatri expressed her views.

"I also like Preity very much. She speaks so sweetly. I will talk to Karan but at the same time, *Ma* you also try," replied Kamini. Gayatri Devi promptly responded, "Surely I will try but Karan is quite close to you. It will be better if you bring up the topic." Sulakshana felt that her efforts would pay, so the discussion ended.

Karan after talking with his aunty that they would be expecting him at the farmhouse made a call after some time to Ashok Vihar as he wanted to talk to his mother. Mudra picked up the phone and he said, "Dear Sis. How are your studies going on? Do you need any help from me?"

"I have taken enough coaching *bhaiya*. Presently I am revising.

If I need your help, I will tell you."

Then Karan asked for his mother and Kamini came on the line, "Karan, how are you, my son? Congratulations on your expected promotion. I could not talk to you earlier because of the guests."

"Thanks, *Ma*, I am fine, and what about all of you?"

"Everyone here is fine. Your grandmother and the others have just left." "I have holidays until Sunday, so I wanted to come to Ashok Vihar but Sulakshana Aunty is insisting that I remain at the farmhouse as she wants me to go to the market with her and wants me to celebrate New Year's Eve here."

Kamini understood perfectly and also wanted Karan to spend more time with Preity.

"Dear son, Sulakshana is your aunt and a guest as well. Moreover, Preity is with her. She wants her to have a good impression of our hospitality. You can come here any time. I will tell your papa about your inability to come," she replied

"So nice of you *Ma*, give my respect to *Papa*, Uncle, and Aunty, and love to the kids."

Karan reached the farmhouse well in time to receive his aunt as he had told her. After dinner when they were sitting in the drawing room laughing over a joke that Karan had told them, Sulakshana said abruptly to him, "Karan tomorrow we intend to go to Connaught Place as Preity has not seen it yet."

"Oh, she has not seen CP yet? It's the most beautiful market the British built in India. We must show it to her. I am ready and at your disposal Aunty." Karan said in a lighter vein.

Premnath said, "Are you taking leave tomorrow, Karan?"

Karan replied, "No sir, my office is closed until Sunday for the New Year. Sulakshana aunty knew that. Monday will be my next working day now."

"That's fine then you accompany them wherever they want."

"I have already committed myself to aunty."

Sulakshana addressed her mother, "Ma you also accompany

us along with uncle to Connaught Place."

"No dear as Preity is going to see CP for the first time you will be walking a lot. It will be better for young people like you to go alone." Sulakshana looked towards her uncle who said, "Your mother is right. You will enjoy yourselves better. I need to devote some time to my writing." Premnath continued "Take the driver with you otherwise Karan will be busy parking the car all the time."

"That's a good idea," Sulakshana replied.

The next day Sohan Lal, Premnath's driver brought the car to the portico and asked Karan, "May I go by the shortest route to CP or by some specific route?"

"Go via Chanakyapuri. I want to show them the diplomatic area."

Sulakshana and Preity got into the back. When Karan opened the front door to sit with the driver Sulakshana said, "Karan come to the back there is a lot of space here." Karan without objecting opened the back door and got in. It was a Honda Accord, a big car with sufficient space. When they were near Kutub Minar, Karan told the driver to stop the car on a side lane and asked the ladies to get out and take an aerial view of the Kutub Minar from a distance. After about five minutes, they continued their journey toward CP. At the AIMS crossing, the driver, instead of going straight to CP via INA market took the left turn to show them Chanakyapuri.

On reaching Chanakyapuri, Karan asked the driver to stop the car. They came out and Preity was impressed to see such a wide road with the embassies of the different countries on both sides. Their next stop was at India Gate. Preity was seeing India Gate for the first time. After ten minutes, they were at Connaught Place. They left the car at Block-A. Karan instructed the driver to park the car at the central parking. He also gave him some money and told him to meet them in the evening at the same point. They moved from the Inner Circle to the Middle Circle and finally to the Outer Circle, looking at the different showrooms and their displays. They entered shops where Sulakshana and Preity wanted to buy something. The weather was excellent, and the sun was enchanting with bright sunlight. In front of the inner circle was a big park with a huge fountain. For some moments of relaxation, they went into the park full of flowers that were swaying in the air redolent with their fragrance and enjoyed a cup of tea. Preity admired the style in which CP was built.

They started wandering around again and when they reached D-Block Karan proposed lunch since it was about 3 p.m. "Would you like some non-vegetarian food or pure vegetarian? We will select the restaurant accordingly."

Both the ladies replied, "Pure vegetarian."

Karan took them to a restaurant that served vegetarian food. They selected their table and Karan placed the order. Preity again said, "I am really enjoying Connaught Place. There is something special in the ambiance which I can't explain but can appreciate."

Karan was happy that Preity liked the area so much. Sulakshana was happy that her niece liked everything around her because of Karan's presence. They relished the food and ice cream and came out for more shopping.

From F-Block they took the short route to A-Block. Sohan Lal saw them and brought the car out of the parking area. They reached the farmhouse late in the evening joking all the way back home.

Premnath and Gayatri were waiting for them, and Sheru served tea as soon as they arrived. Preity told them all about her impressions and experiences. Karan called Vinod to join them. Vinod knew most of Gayatri's relatives but would join family gatherings only when invited to do so. He told many stories and jokes with a touch of Shayari in such an interesting manner that everyone who knew him felt his absence if he was not there.

The next day was New Year's Eve. Premnath and Gayatri Devi wanted to celebrate it on a large scale. She invited her sons and their families from Ashok Vihar. Kamini was initially reluctant due to Mudra's studies but agreed finally with an understanding that they would reach the farmhouse late in the evening. Both the ladies also understood that participating in such celebrations would help her psychologically in her preparations for coming examinations. She rang her younger daughter-in-law, Sunanda, and invited the family as well. Premnath suggested calling his chartered accountant friend, Kamal Kapoor, and his wife. Gayatri liked the couple very much, so she asked her brother to speak to his friend without losing further time as people normally fixed such programs in advance and they were already late. Premnath invited his friend with his wife in the next few minutes. Then Karan suggested, "Should we involve our staff in the celebrations."

Premnath promptly said, "Why not? We should also distribute new clothes as we did on Diwali."

It was decided that clothes would be distributed to the staff at an evening tea to which all occupants of the farmhouse would be invited. Gayatri suggested, "Why not encourage the staff to celebrate New Year's Eve at the staff hall together? And dinner can be served to them from the common kitchen." This idea was also appreciated by the gathering. Gayatri added, "I think there is a lot of work for Karan and Vinod to do tomorrow buying everything for the dinner."

"We are ready and will go to the market early in the morning." Both Karan and Vinod said.

Gayatri added, "Vinod, I think an extra cook is needed if it can be arranged easily." Gayatri's aim was to give Rajaram and Revati, the cooks, some respite so that they too could enjoy the celebrations with others

"That arrangement will be made Grandma."

CHAPTER 21

Everyone was busy with the preparations for the night. Gayatri Devi went with her daughter and Preity to Green Park Market to buy gifts for the staff. Karan and Vinod went to get the vegetables, fruit, milk, and other food stuffs according to the list prepared by Rajaram. Since the area in the staff hall would be insufficient, Vinod placed an order for two beautiful tents and some furniture and temporary lighting arrangements in the tent house. The tent house employees were waiting for them at the farmhouse by the time Karan and Vinod returned. They told them where to put up the tents. They were arranged so that one entrance would be from the staff hall, the second facing the staff quarters, and the third one from the gallery connected to the dining room via the office room. Gayatri Devi and Premnath liked the idea of putting up the tent, as it was bitterly cold. By about 5 p.m., everything was ready. Vinod requested Gayatri Devi to make a final round to satisfy herself that all was in order. On her instructions, the gifts, which were packed and had the individual names written on them by Shobha, were placed on the tables laid out in the tents. It was decided to start the evening program with the staff at about 6.30 p.m.

Gayatri Devi had instructed Shobha the day before to tell all staff members about the function, which she did within ten minutes. Shobha also told her mother when she went to her quarters that night. Her mother reacted happily, and then asked her daughter, "Earlier only Diwali was celebrated like this, now this function is also being celebrated?"

"They celebrated this function earlier also, but late at night.

This time they are also celebrating it separately in the evening with the staff." Shobha continued, "I think it may be Karan Babu's idea. He is so nice to all the people working as staff. I am still not sure why we have been invited."

All the staff was curious as to why they were invited on a day other than Diwali, but they were happy. When they arrived with their families Shobha informed Gayatri Devi. The entire family along with Vinod were with the staff within five minutes. Gayatri said something in Shobha's ear and within a few minutes, she unpacked snacks and tea was served to all. Premnath and Gayatri were close to their staff and moved around amongst them, asking questions about their children, etc. Gayatri, who normally maintained a distance from others, so that she could get the work done efficiently, now became part of the gathering. This was her unique quality, which her brother always appreciated. It looked a bit strange to Preity that Karan was close to everyone working in the farmhouse and was even cracking jokes with them. One child sang a song and another recited a poem, which everyone appreciated with applause. Then Premnath and Gayatri Devi came to the table where the gifts were placed.

Premnath said, "It was Karan's idea to celebrate New Year's Eve like Diwali. We all liked the idea, so we are here to celebrate the occasion with all of you. Thank you all for coming." Amidst the applause that followed, Premnath and Gayatri started distributing the gifts. When this process was over, Gayatri told the gathering, "I hope you will enjoy the music which Vinod has arranged. Rajaram and Revati have made dinner for you all, so don't go before it is served." There was clapping again and Gayatri Devi, Premnath, and the others took their leave. No guest had arrived yet, but they were expecting them at any time. Vijay and Ramesh Malhotra with their respective families arrived as first guests. Next Kamal Kapoor came, Premnath's school friend and business advisor, along with his wife, Madhu, an author. The couple was regular visitors to the farmhouse over the last twenty years. They rarely refused an invitation for coming there. They had tried their best to make Premnath marry again with the help of Prem's parents and sister, as they knew the entire family.

Premnath was reluctant to marry for a second time due to the bad experience of his first marriage. He also feared that his old parents would bear the mercy of a new lady. After his parent's demise, the Kapoors tried again, but Prem told them that he was too old to marry. In the end, they had to give up their attempts, but their friendship and business relations remained as cordial as ever.

Premnath visited Kapoor's office three or four times a year. He was only called when there was some important business investment to be made, as Kapoor gave great importance to Premnath's intuitive business acumen, even though the basic information was collected by Kapoor's office.

Premnath and Gayatri were also regular visitors to Kamal Kapoor's home at Defense Colony, in South Delhi.

Premnath had told the Kapoors to bring the necessary clothes as they were supposed to stay at the farmhouse that night. On Gayatri's suggestion, two waiters were hired from the tent house, and they were now serving the guests snacks, soups, and drinks.

Light music was played in the background and there was a lot of noise and laughter in the hall. There was sufficient sitting space for everyone and alcohol was also served. Karan and Vinod tried to avoid it, but Kapoor forced them, as it was New Year's Eve. The seating arrangement was organized so that the men could sit separately from the women to enjoy their drinks and the women could talk more freely amongst themselves.

Madhu Kapoor was chatting with Sulakshana while kamini, Sunanda, and Preity were silent listeners. Gayatri Devi slipped out for a few minutes to check the arrangement. Karan and Vinod finished their drinks and excusing themselves, joined

Gayatri Devi in her round of the kitchen and tents. She was happy to see the house staff enjoying themselves. Moreover, she was satisfied that Shobha was taking care of both sides. She made a round upstairs to check the sleeping arrangements for the guests.

On returning to the party, Vinod and Karan were persuaded by the others to make themselves another glass of whisky. Kamal Kapoor started questioning his friend, "When are you intending to finish your book?"

"You mean my new book! Perhaps by the middle of this year well if, everything goes well." Then Kapoor started a new topic, "You know in the last twenty years wherever my friend has invested, it has turned into gold. I give him information on several reasonably good proposals when he is ready to invest. He selects one or two, but whichever he selects turns into gold."

Karan said with amazement, "Is that so uncle?" Premnath laughingly replied, "No, no! He is joking."

Kapoor contradicted Nath saying, "I am not joking at all. I started following Premnath's intuitive judgment for my own investments too and now get better returns from my investments."

Karan joked, "But Kapoor Uncle, you are my granduncle's investment advisor and chartered accountant. How does this reversal of roles materialize?"

"Well, you may say that but based on my experience, I give value to his final judgment on the investments though the base work of collecting the data and making the proposals is done by my company. My friend is gifted in this, and I want you all to have the benefit of his talents which I am sure are only God gifted." He continued, "Vinod who is a regular visitor to my office knows this fact too and has invested his small savings based on Premnath's judgments, but perhaps the rest of you do not know this."

Vijay and Ramesh both exclaimed that they never knew this about their uncle. Kamal Kapoor added, "Don't think I am breaking my friend's confidence to anyone. Never! I am committed by oath to maintaining my clients' confidence. Whatever Vinod knows too, is a result of his work with Premnath but I am happy he also keeps the secrets like a true private secretary."

At this, Vinod felt embarrassed and said, "Whatever I am doing, Sir, it is my job. If I talk about my boss's investments to other people, then I am not competent to be his private secretary."

Kapoor clarified further, "That's why you have outgrown your status and I have every respect for your integrity. Premnath also considers you a family member."

They heard Gayatri Devi calling them to the dining table for dinner.

Premnath asked whether the children had eaten and Gayatri told him that they had. The music that Vinod had organized was still being played.

Shobha was there to look after everything and Gayatri asked her whether the staff had their dinner.

Shobha replied, "Yes Madam they have all eaten."

The hired waiters were serving the dinner and Sheru and Champa were also present. Sulakshana played her game again. She asked Karan to sit next to Preity while she sat opposite her. The ladies were requested to sit first, and the men had selected their seats accordingly. The food consisted of North Indian and South Indian dishes. Both Rajaram and Revati were South Indians, but they had worked in the north for more than eighteen years, and now they were experts in both types of cuisines. Madhu Kapoor could not resist herself and said, "Whenever we eat at the farmhouse, we talk about it for days." Gayatri replied, "I am happy you like the food."

Sulakshana also agreed with Madhu and said, "Mama today the food is excellent. I think I am overeating."Gayatri smiled at her daughter's comments.

After dinner, they returned to the sofas. The men and women sat in one group now. Sulakshana took the lead and proposed, "Let us start a musical game. Each one of us will sing a few lines of a song which he or she likes."

"That's a good idea." Premnath seconded Sulakshana's suggestions.

Kapoor asked, 'What if someone doesn't know a song or is not comfortable singing?"

"Then he or she can tell a joke," Sulakshana responded.

Everyone agreed with Sulakshana's proposal. The next point was where to start, and Sulakshana resolved it by starting. Next came Madhu Kapoor, who sang the latest popular song. Then one by one Kapoor, Vinod, and Vijay cracked jokes. Vijay related a joke on Akbar and Birbal and Karan, Preity, Ramesh, Sunanda, and kamini all sang a few lines from the popular film songs. Gayatri and Prem sang old hits from the films. Then came the demand for dancing. Premnath suggested, "Now I think the youngest amongst us should do something."

It was unanimously agreed that Vinnie, Ishu, and Mudra would dance with Karan and Preity. Vinod changed the music and played the latest Hindi Punjabi pop and raised the volume. The elders enjoyed seeing their youngsters and Sulakshana's eyes were observing her mother and sister-in-law when they were looking at Preity and Karan dancing together with the other's youngsters. At exactly midnight the lights were put off for a few seconds and when they came on again everyone wished each other a happy New Year.

It was Karan and Vinod's responsibility to show the guest's the arrangements for their bedrooms. Karan's room was allotted to his parents. Mr. and Mrs. Kapoor were given the room above

Vinod's room in the front. As there were four bedrooms upstairs, Sulakshana, who was staying with Preity in the room opposite Karan's original room shifted for one night to her mother's room downstairs. Preity continued in the same room for that night with Mudra. The room next to Priety's was given to Ramesh Malhotra and his family, with an extra bed for the kids.

Karan and Vinod came downstairs. Karan was asked to sleep in Premnath's room so after saying good night to Vinod he went there. When Karan entered the room, he saw his granduncle sitting in meditation.

Without disturbing him he slowly moved to the empty bed. There was a dim light on so Karan lay down in his bed. As soon as he was in bed thoughts of Reena engulfed him and he started thinking about her. After a few minutes he heard his granduncle's voice, "Are you feeling sleepy, Karan?"

"Well not exactly Sir, I did not disturb you as you were meditating."

"Thanks. Actually, I want to discuss a matter of importance, but if you are feeling sleepy we can talk another time."

"I am quite awake Sir."

"All right then, listen. I want to make a will. I want this farmhouse to continue as a farmhouse as it is now, welcoming relatives and maintaining it as it is after my demise." Premnath stopped.

Karan questioned, "What is the difficulty in doing so?"

"The problem is who will maintain it the way I want." After a pause, he continued "I can see only one person who can do it and that person is you. You can maintain it even after me or when I am very old if I survive for that long."

Karan tried to get clarification, "What do you want exactly Sir?"

"I want to make a will in your name so that you become the owner of the farmhouse after my death, but I also want you to maintain it as it is being maintained now, which I am sure you will." After exposing his inner most feelings, Premnath looked toward Karan and waited for his reply. Karan kept quiet for a few minutes and then said, "I will fulfill your desire to the extent that this farmhouse will remain a sort of guest house for relatives and maintain its ecology, keeping its greenery, plants, and flowers blooming as it is now, but Sir I can't accept its ownership. That is against my concept of things."

After a few minutes, Premnath said, "I knew in the core of my heart that this would be your reply. One day I spoke to your grandmother about this. She also felt you would give this sort of reply. I have another idea if you like to listen now, or we may talk some other time?"

"Well, Sir I will listen now if you want to tell me."

"All right then, I am going to explain what the other alternative is. I want to create a Trust. My sister or I will be the chairperson of the trust as long as one of us is alive. After that I want you to become the chairperson and continue looking after the farmhouse with the income I will specify and keep separately. I also want Vinod to join you as member secretary of the trust after my demise. I want you to become a member of the trust after it is formed. I want the chairperson to be empowered to nominate members, but not more than one from each family. We will write the constitution of the trust after thorough deliberations in which I want you to participate. We will take care of the legal and financial aspects according to the law of the land to make the constitution flawless."

Karan could see his granduncle's face, which looked quite satisfied so he replied, "I have no objection Sir to be the caretaker of the farmhouse even in the capacity of the chairperson of the trust."

"Well, I am really very happy to hear this. I was expecting such a reply from a rational person like you," said Premnath Karan smiled, "Thank you Sir for your appreciative comments about me,"and both slept peacefully after that.

At about 8 a.m., Gayatri peeped into Premnath's room and found them both sleeping, so she did not disturb them.

When Premnath and Karan came to the table for breakfast it was around 10 o'clock in the morning. The Kapoor and Malhotra families who had eaten breakfast earlier were chatting amongst themselves. Gayatri said that Sulakshana, Preity, Mudra, and both her grandsons were coming down shortly.

Premnath spoke smilingly to her, "That means we are not so late; at least a few others will join us shortly for breakfast."

Gayatri clarified, "I have had my breakfast with the guests so that they feel comfortable."

Premnath replied, "Sister you did a good thing." Premnath was just saying this when Sulakshana and the other came down the stairs. After wishing good morning to each other, when Sulakshana heard that they had already eaten, she took their permission to join her uncle and Karan at the breakfast table. Gayatri said to her daughter, "Dear please start. Both Premnath and Karan are waiting for you."

While eating breakfast Sulakshana spoke to her mother, "We want to go to Karol Bagh today to buy some men's clothes and jewelry. Will you accompany us?"

Gayatri Devi replied, "Sorry dear I may not be able to accompany you. It will be better if you ask Karan. These days we are bothering him too much."

On hearing this Karan said, "Grandma, Aunty is here only for today.

Tomorrow she is going back. I have no problem accompanying her to Karol Bagh. Moreover, Kohli Jewellers at Karol Bagh are very well known to me. My friend has joined his father in his jewelry business."

Sulakshana promptly replied, "What could be better than that! At least we can rely on the person from whom we are going to purchase diamond and gold ornaments."

"Yes not only will you get a fair deal, but you may also get a discount."

After breakfast, they joined the Kapoors and Malhotras and cracked a few jokes together. The Kapoors were ready to leave and the Malhotras followed suit.

In the evening Sulakshana came back from Karol Bagh very happy with theday's purchases, "Karan's friend gave us a good discount. They have a big shop of the latest fashioned gold and diamond jewelry."

"Thank God! You are satisfied." Gayatri Devi expressed happily while looking at the jewelry."

As usual Reena's thoughts came to Karan as soon as he lay down on the bed. There was a feeling of excitement as she was coming back from Kolkata the next day. He bought a cellular phone but could not talk to Reena as her mobile was yet to be charged which she intended to do on coming back to Delhi. Vivek had a mobile phone, so Karan talked to him. He wished Vivek and his other friends a happy New Year. During the last three or four days, he had become comfortable with Preity, but he considered her as a friend of the same age group. Karan's behavior had become more mature since he had given his heart to Reena. It was clearly love at first sight. With the passage of time after his first meeting with her, he had developed into a more emotionally balanced person. Feelings of love increased his respect for the fair sex. He recalled his earlier younger days when he used to get attracted to most of the young girls and sometimes even to those older than him. A few of such attractions disturbed his studies or even his interest in games of his choice like badminton and tennis. In spite of his lack of concentration, he managed well in both studies and games, but he could not excel in either, even though he had the ability. His attractions continued but he never developed a particular interest in anyone until he met Reena. In Reena, his interest went deep and his love for her was intense. The result of these intense feelings was that he lost his habit of getting attracted to every other girl. Even during the early days, the idea of exploiting fair sex never crossed his mind. He had respect for women. The best part of his personality was that he was never abusive even when he was angry. Making cheap comments about the opposite sex was unacceptable to him. Still, he was not a dull person. He felt the romance in his veins and now all his romantic thoughts were for one girl. Perhaps in such a state of mind, even a beautiful girl like Preity could not make any headway into his heart. Had he met her a few months earlier when he had not come across Reena, he might have got attracted to her, but only as an attraction for the opposite sex, certainly not for love.

Before leaving for Jalandhar, Sulakshana again impressed upon her mother to talk to Karan directly or through his mother. Karan intended to go to Ashok Vihar as soon as Sulakshana and Preity were leaving the place. Gayatri planned it in her own way and when Karan was at breakfast a bit earlier than usual, because he knew his aunt was going to catch the 10 a.m. Shatabadi Express, she asked him, "Why don't you also come to the station to see your aunty off? In that case, I can also go to Ashok Vihar with you, and we will come back in the evening." The idea appealed to Karan. Gayatri Devi wanted to talk to kamini about Preity.

At the New Delhi Railway Station, the scene was emotional. Both the mother and the daughter had tears in their eyes. Karan rarely saw tears in his grandmother's eyes. Her strict disciplinary image was shattered. Gayatri kissed her daughter several times. She also kissed Preity. Karan bade farewell by touching his aunt's feet, and she responded by kissing her nephew's forehead. Preity shook hands with him and made him to promise for visiting Jalandhar.

CHAPTER 22

Within the next forty minutes, grandmother and grandson were with their family at Ashok Vihar. After the preliminary greetings and light snacks, Gayatri, Kamini, and Sunanda went to another room. Karan was with his uncle and father, as Mudra was studying, and Vinnie and Ishu went out to play cricket. Cricket is the rage in schools and colleges all over India during the winter. They play cricket everywhere, not only on cricket fields but even on the roadsides of residential areas, especially on Sundays and holidays.

Karan's father asked his son, "When exactly will you get your promotion?"

"I must go to Mumbai next week for about three to four weeks for aproject. I hope to get my promotion on my return."

"What will be your designation?" asked Ramesh.

"My initial post was that of consultant. The company changed it to Assistant Manager, because of some reorganization. After the promotion, I will be designated Manager."

"Yes, our company had also done a similar type of reorganization last year."

In the other room, Gayatri was with her daughters-in-law listening to the news about the neighbors. She was one of those lucky ladies who had good relations with her daughters-in-law. She changed the topic and said to Kamini, "Preity seems a decent girl and quite beautiful, although a bit fashionable. If you would like her as your future daughter-in-law, then do talk to Karan at the earliest possible."

"I will be happy if Karan agrees to Preity. I shall try to talk to him today after lunch." She hurried off to the kitchen to get lunch ready. Gayatri and Sunanda joined her to help.

After lunch, Karan was resting in a room adjacent to his parent's bedroom. His mother came in and asked him, "Karan how do you like Preity?"

"Ma, why are you asking? She is a beautiful girl and very nice. That's all"

"No, that's not all. I want to know more. If you like her then we can talk to her parents about an engagement between the two of you." Kamini said in one breath.

Looking bewildered at first and then controlling himself he said, "*Ma*, liking Preity does not mean I want to marry her."

"But you must marry someone. You are going to be twenty-five years old and well settled in your job. If we start now, it will take another six months to one year for your marriage to take place." Karan understood his mother's feelings, so he said politely, "*Ma* I may end up marrying this year but please give me time to decide about the girl."

"Who is stopping you from deciding? The way you speak it appears as if you have a girl in mind."

Karan was initially at a loss to find a reply to his mother's query but then managed to say, "Well at present I am not able to affirm what you have said. Give me some more time Ma; you will get a reply to all your queries."

"All right then, give me a reply within the next few days," Kamini said smiling lovingly and kissing her son on his forehead.

Karan was about to tell his mother about Reena, but something stopped him from doing so. He preferred to talk to Reena in person first and get more unformation about her family's views on the affair before telling anyone in his family.

He was so busy in the office all morning on Monday, that he did not even have time for a cup of tea. Now he felt his work was nearly complete and his eyes went automatically to his watch. It was half an hour before lunch, so he dropped the idea of having tea and decided to wait for lunch. His phone rang and Reena was on the line.

"Hello Karan, it is Reena how are you?"

"I am well, what about you? Are you speaking from Kolkata or Delhi?" "I am fine, thank you. We arrived from Kolkata yesterday evening. I am calling from my college and will go to South Extension to get my mobile charged. Can you come there for some time so that we can talk?"

Karan thought for a moment and said, "I can come in about half an hour and can stay with you for about an hour. We can have lunch together."

"All right, that's fine. You will find me near the same restaurant where we met earlier."

Karan walked towards the restaurant at South Extension and found Reena waiting for him. His heart started thumping as he walked up to her and he managed somehow to control himself, but could not judge what Reena was feeling. They shook hands and went inside the restaurant. Karan found a small table vacant, and both proceeded toward it.

"May I just look at you for a few seconds before we talk?" Karan said emotionally.

"Why? I am dying to talk to you, and you want me to wait!" Reena said smiling.

"Don't talk about dying, even when it means something different." Karan said and continued, "Have you got your mobile charged?"

"Yes, just a few minutes ago."

"Then note down my number and tell me yours."

Karan smiled and said, "Suddenly a mobile is worthwhile.

Earlier I considered it useful only for the business community." And continued "Now tell me what the status of our friendship with your parents is, and why is it that your father must talk to your uncle before giving his affirmation to you?"

"It may appear a bit strange, but the fact is my dad is under my uncle's obligation." Reena took a pause then explained, "When he came back to India after voluntary retirement his brother offered him a partnership in his well-established export business and handed over my father's portion of the farmhouse, which was well maintained and ready to move into when our family came. He is of the view that these days, brothers don't do so much for each other. He believes that since his brother has done so much for him, and being older, it is his duty to tell him about this proposal and get his approval to go ahead." Reena waited for Karan's reaction.

"I understand now, but tell me, when will he talk to your uncle?"

"Today, my parents will go to my uncle's house to talk about the issue.

My parents have no objection to our relationship at all. I hope my uncle will also agree with them."

"I hope it is so," Karan replied.

Lunch was served and they started eating without speaking. After lunch, Karan looked at his watch and then said, "I think I should leave now. Please call me to let me know what has happened."

Karan paid the bill and they went out. They shook hands again and went in different directions to their vehicles.

After he met with Reena, Karan felt reassured that her parents would consent to their friendship, subject to the approval of her uncle. After his talk with Reena, her father's view point that he should get his brother's approval before giving his formal consent also seemed quite valid. He felt that the matter was cleared, and he felt contented and happy. Although Reena had told him all this on the telephone from Kolkata, he was doubtful about what had been the real outcome of her talk with her parents.

Then after meeting Reena and talking face to face with her, things seemed more logical to him. He felt that he could at least give some hint to his mother and grandmother since they were both so eager about his marriage. He decided to tell them that very day.

That evening, feeling in such a happy mood, he hugged his grandmother who was reading a magazine. Gayatri Devi responded with equal warmth and said, "Karan my dear son, you look very happy. May I know the good news?"

Instead of replying, Karan asked, "Where is granduncle?"

Gayatri replied, "Mr. Varma came here and has taken him to his farmhouse for some consultations. But tell me why you are so happy."

Karan reprimanded himself that he could not suppress his feelings but seeing his grandmother looking at him with such expectations in her eyes, he told the truth, "Grandma I am happy today. It is because of a green signal from the family of a girl whom I have loved for some time.

"Is that so? Who is the lucky girl? Please tell me at once."

"Dear Grandma she is our neighbor, Reena."

"She is Reena! That sweet Bengali beauty! Oh, my dear Karan I just can't believe my ears. Please tell me how long you have loved each other." Gayatri Devi expressed her happiness and surprise at the same time. "She was coming here talking to you, me and your granduncle, being friendly with everyone. You don't know how much I like the girl! Strangely, though, I never thought that both of you have started loving each other."

Karan was ready with his reply by the time his grandmother finished her emotional outpourings. He said, "Dear Grandma I wanted to tell you earlier, but due to the presence of Aunt Sulakshana, and also Reena not being quite clear about her family's reaction, I could not. It is only today that she has cleared the matter from her side."

Her next query was, 'Where does the matter stand now? Has she told her parents? And what is their reaction?"

Karan clarified, "Actually she promised to tell her parents in Kolkata and I was waiting for their consent."

"I see! Now I understand! You wanted to tell us only after she got the green signal from her parents. I appreciate that."

Karan was happy that his grandmother was satisfied with his act of not telling her earlier.

She next asked Karan,

"Have you told your mother?"

"Not yet."

"Please tell her at once."

"All right Grandma I am going to my room, and I will tell her."

Karan went to his bedroom, picked up the phone, and after the initial chit chat between mother and son, told her about Reena. His mother's reaction was like his grandmother's. She also liked Reena very much when she met her at Sulakshana's birthday party. She never thought of Reena as her daughter-in-law because she was Bengali and also very rich. Hearing that from her son, she was extremely happy which surprised her son. He asked her to inform his father, uncle, and aunt.

When Karan came downstairs, Gayatri asked him if he had spoken to his mother. On getting his reply, she said, "I want to tell Premnath who will be very happy to hear this."

When Premnath and Vinod sat down for dinner with Gayatri and Karan, Gayatri said, "I have some good news."

Premnath said promptly, "What is it? Let us hear it."

"Karan has selected a girl for himself. They both love each other."

Premnath and Vinod congratulated Karan by shaking hands. Karan thanked them with a big smile. Vinod who knew about the affair kept quiet. Premnath asked, "Who is the lucky girl? Do we know her or not?"

Gayatri replied, "Yes dear you know her very well. She was your student." Gayatri paused to see her brother's reaction, who said with amazement and a smile, "Is she Reena? That beautiful, intelligent doll? Am I right?"

Gayatri Devi could not resist herself and said, "Yes, she is Reena, our girl next door."

Premnath said happily, "That's wonderful news. The idea did come to mymind that Reena is a good match for Karan, but I refrained from saying anything. I am delighted with this news."

Vinod played his part well by not showing any advance knowledge of the affair. He just smiled along with everyone else.

When Karan and Vinod went to their rooms, Gayatri Devi told Premnath the details about Reena's parent's views and that he is still waiting for the final consent due to her uncle's approval as informed by Karan. Premnath felt that the senior Mr. Mukherji would give his consent.

Reena's parents decided to visit the senior Mr. Mukherji to get his consent about the marriage between Reena and Karan. Karan had already made it clear to Reena that he was not going to accept any dowry; not even the routine one. Reena told her parents to inform her uncle about Karan's rare quality of not accepting dowry of any kind.

As soon as Subhash and Rakhi reached the lawn where Mr. and Mrs. Subhodh Mukherji were sitting, Subhodh said loudly, "*Lo*, Subhash and Rakhi have come. I was coming to your side to give you some good news."

"What is the good news?" Both Subhash and Rakhi said in unison.

Subodh said, "There is a very good offer for Reena from my friend's family. They are very rich Bengalis. The family saw Reena at our son's marriage. The boy is an MBA from the USA." He pointed toward his wife and continued "I was just telling your sister-in-law about the offer. The good part is that the boy is coming to India on Friday. He will be joining his father's business which is exporting complete projects to the Middle East and Eastern Europe."

On hearing this, both Subhash and Rakhi found themselves in a difficult position. They looked at each other. Darkness was descending and it helped them to hide their expressions. Subhash, not wanting to expose their unhappiness on hearing the news, said to his brother, "That's good news. Let Reena and the boy decide if they like each other."

"Yes, yes. I told my friend Shanker Gonguly very clearly that we will go ahead only if the boy and the girl like each other."

Subhash and Rakhi were a bit relieved on hearing this. The matter was not final, and the decision would lie with their daughter.

Reena was desperately waiting for her parents to return, but the outcome of the meeting increased her desperation and she started crying. Looking at the effect of their talk, Subhash tried to console his daughter, "My dear, don't worry. I assure you that your mother and I are with you. Please understand my difficult situation. I just want a positive signal for Karan from your uncle. Regarding this boy coming from the USA, you need not worry. Just reject him, but please go through the formalities as your uncle wants." Rakhi during all this time was hugging and encouraging her daughter. Subhash Mukherji looked at his daughter waiting for her reaction who said with choked emotions "Papa! How will you pursue the matter about

Karan…?

"Dear, don't worry now, when the present issue with this boy is over, I will talk to *Dada* about Karan and tell him clearly how much both of you like each other. I expect him to agree as he loves you so much."

Her mother, added, "Let this situation with the new boy get over. We will take up the matter with your uncle seriously and without any further delay."

Reena felt a bit reassured. She wondered whether to tell Karan immediately on his mobile but had a second thought and decided to tell him the next day.

During dinner at the Nath's farmhouse, Karan announced, "I am going to Mumbai for about three to four weeks from Monday."

Gayatri asked Karan "Is Monday confirmed?"

"Yes, Grandma the program is fixed. I will get the air tickets from theoffice tomorrow."

Gayatri Devi then said, "Savitri Devi's niece is coming here for about two weeks on Wednesday. She must appear for an interview in Delhi. She will stay with us."

Premnath said, "I remember Savitri Devi stayed here after her retirement, many years ago for a few days." she contradicted her brother, by smiling and then said, "She stayed for more than a month here at the farmhouse to collect her retirement benefits, not for a few days. She was my colleague and close friend who went to Lucknow to join her brother, as she never married." Gayatri continued, "Savitri's niece is a teacher by profession. She also writes poetry in Hindi. She is not married though she is around twenty-eight years old. While her aunt was in Delhi, she visited her number of times."

The next day Karan received a message from Reena that she would meet him at a particular spot near his office during his lunch break. He was anxiously waiting to hear about the meeting between Reena's parents and uncle.

When they met, Karan suggested going to a restaurant for lunch. After placing their order, Reena informed him about the previous day's developments. Karan was worried, but she assured him with her parent's words. It was clear though that Reena's parents were in favor of their relationship but the circumstances of those days did not favor dialogue between the brothers, which would materialize ultimately. He suggested Reena meet the boy as her parents were on her side. He then told her reluctantly, that he was going to Mumbai for about three weeks. He skipped the words 'three to four weeks' as even telling her that he was going for three weeks seemed to him like a very long time. She looked so sad that Karan felt necessary to reassure her. So he said to her, "Dear please, don't worry at all. Just think I am here with you. In case of any emergency or problem, just call me and I will come here without any delay."

With such emotionally charged words, she felt somewhat reassured. Karan was busy preparing for Mumbai during the next two days. On the second day, he went straight to Ashok Vihar from the office to meet his parents before leaving for Mumbai. His father was satisfied with the first information about Reena, but his mother questioned him in such detail, that at times it was difficult for him to reply. He told his mother that Reena's family was like a joint family and his father had to get the consent of his elder brother on major family decisions. He convinced his mother that things would be finalized only on his return from Mumbai.

Karan's flight was on Sunday evening, so he returned to the farmhouse before noon. His luggage was already packed. He went straight to his grandmother who was enjoying the sunny day on the front lawn. She asked him about any developments and he told her the same thing that he had told his mother.

Karan sat in the aircraft and thought of Reena. He wondered how she would handle the situation with the boy with whom she was to meet the next evening. All he could do was pray for her to manage that difficult situation with flying colors.

A company functionary, Mr. Mehta, received Karan at Mumbai Airport. He was to stay at the company guest house on Linking Road in Bandra. Theguest house was situated in a prime locality with plenty of hustle and bustle around. The Catering services were provided from early morning till late night at the guesthouse.

Karan ate his breakfast the next morning and was ready at 9 a.m. when thephone rang. It was Mr. Mehta, who asked, "Sir at what time shall I send the car for you?"

"I am ready, you may send it now."

Within fifteen minutes, Karan was in the company car going to their office. He returned late in the evening. After a hot bath, he put on casual clothes and switched on the TV. His mobile rang at that moment. Reena was on the other side. Karan without much formality asked about her meeting with the boy from the US. To calm his anxiety, Reena told him in a few words that she had succeeded in her aim. She asked Karan to give her his landline number and said she would call him on that phone to give him the details within the next few minutes. Karan was waiting desperately for her call, but at least her success with the meeting soothed his nerves.

The landline phone rang after about ten minutes. He picked up the phoneexcitedly and said, "Why did you change from mobile to landline?"

"I wanted to talk in more details, for which you would have been unnecessarily charged."

"Oh, I see! Now you have started trying to save my money like a good wife. Please tell me the details. What happened?"

'It has gone well. As soon as we were alone, I told him clearly that I liked someone else. The boy was not shocked at all, as I was expecting him to be. Instead, he told me that he also came there under pressure from his father and did not want to marry so early, just after completing his studies. He further conveyed that he was thinking of changing his mind after he saw me but after my response, he would also stick to his original decision. It was then settled between us that he would be telling his parents that he did not like me. It seemed that the boy was a thorough gentleman.'

She waited for some moments then expressed her feeling to him, "I also admire you for showing so much courage." After some sweet talks between the lovers, they disconnected the phones. Karan then made two calls one to his mother and the other one to his grandmother informing them of his well-being.

CHAPTER 23

On Tuesday evening, when Premnath and Gayatri were having their tea on the front lawns she said to her brother, "I got a call from Lucknow by Savitri, my friend said that her niece, Archana, will be arriving tomorrow by the Shatabadi Express."

"It's nice! Should I send Vinod with the driver to bring her from the station or would you like to go with Vinod?"

"I have been feeling a bit unwell due to a bad cold since the morning. It'sbetter if Vinod manages this independently."

At that time Vinod was in his office so Premnath called him on the intercom, requesting him to join them. He conveyed to Vinod, "Dear you have to go to the railway station tomorrow to fetch a guest." He was given the train and the coach number. The question then arose as to how Vinod and the guest would recognize each other. Gayatri solved the problem by calling her friend to ask about the details of the dress her niece would be wearing and told her about Vinod's clothes (after confirming from him),build, height, and that he would wear a yellow rose in his coat pocket.

Gayatri Devi and Savitri Devi worked in the same school at Model Town. Savitri was junior to Gayatri by about two years, and they were good friends. When Gayatri was transferred to the school at RK Puram, Savitri became the principal of Model Town School, but their friendship continued.

Archana had visited Delhi twice before when her aunt was in service. The first time she came, she was a school girl and Gayatri was still working in Model Town. Since Gayatri and Savitri, both lived in Ashok Vihar, Gayatri met Archana often and became very fond of her. Archana received loads of presents and a lot of affection from Gayatri Devi. On her second visit, Gayatri was living at the farmhouse. She went to Ashok Vihar, especially to meet Archana, and stayed at Savitri's house for a day. Archana, by then was in college. Plans were made for her to visit Gayatri at the farmhouse, but due to one reason or another, it did not materialize. Gayatri went twice to Lucknow with Savitri to visit her parents, while they were alive. During the last six years, the friends could not meet each other but had been talking regularly on the phone.

Archana was very close to her Aunt Savitri. She wrote poems in Hindi which were published regularly in Lucknow Newspapers and a few leading magazines. She was a Hindi language teacher in a public school. She was twenty-eight years old but not married. She was beautiful, tall, and slim, and a few offers for marriage came to her parents, but she refused all of them. When asked if she was going to be like her aunt who never married, she always replied in the negative. The fact was that she had not found a person of her choice. She was the youngest child of her parents, and her two brothers and a sister were married. As both of her brothers were in service outside Lucknow, she lived with her parents. Her Aunt Savitri Devi lived in a separate house next door to her brother's. Archana was coming to Delhi for an interview with a renowned Hindi language publisher for a middle-level job in its editorial department to fulfill her creative urge. As her taste was more inclined to the literary side, she wanted to change from a teaching job to an editorial one. She had convinced Savitri to stay with her in Delhi if she would get the job.

Vinod reached the Railway station well in time. He waited at the exit gate.

He was confident of recognizing the girl because of the description he was given. After the train stopped, he saw a girl about two carriages away from him wearing a suit of the color he was told Archana would be wearing. He rushed up to her and said, "Good morning, Miss." Vinod was expecting a hearty response from the girl but she just looked at him. Vinod said, "Miss I am from Nath's farmhouse. Madam Gayatri Devi is waiting for you," but there was no response. Then a young man came towards her and she responded enthusiastically to him. Vinod slipped away hurriedly, realizing itwas a mistaken identity. He returned to the exit gate and started looking at the passengers. He realized his folly of moving away from the gate.

Archana was looking around for a gentleman in a dark grey suit with ayellow rose in his breast pocket. She waited at the exit gate for about two minutes, and then she went out, giving her ticket to the ticket collector standing near the gate.

Archana glanced around but no one in a dark grey suit with a yellow rose was visible. Archana was perplexed, but then collecting her courage, she went towards the STD booth to make a phone call to the farmhouse. Her luggage was with the porter who was moving along with her. She was about to speak to the operator, when she heard, "Excuse me, Miss, are you Ms. Archana from Lucknow? I am from the Nath farmhouse." She turned around and to her relief saw that the person addressing her had a yellow rose in his pocket. "Yes, I am Archana." When Archana looked at his face, she found a mature young man standing in front of her. Vinod's relief and happiness returned to him when he realized that he had found the lost Archana. She was more beautiful than he expected and looking intently at her he explained, "Miss I am Vinod, Mr. Nath's private secretary."

Archana looked at the well-mannered, matured young man and extended her hand toward him. He responded by shaking her hand. Archana said with pleasant surprise, 'Thank God you are here. Now my worries are over."

Vinod asked the porter to follow them to the car. Vinod paid him and opened the back door of the car and asked Archana to enter the car. Vinod was about to sit in front with the driver, when Archana said to him, "Please come to the back seat so that I get some information about the farmhouse and the place where I have to appear for the interview."

"Oh, sure Miss," Vinod replied. He got into the back seat and instructed Sohan Lal to drive to the farmhouse.

Archana started the conversation, "What exactly do you do as a private secretary? I don't know much about it."

"Well, Mr. Nath is a renowned author, and he has a good fan mail which I attend to." Next time Archana said, "I heard from my aunt that Prem uncle is a scholar and architect by profession. He worked in the US and earned a lot of money. Frankly speaking, it's news to me that he is a renowned author."

"He is writing his third book and I am helping him by providing information according to his requirements from the Internet. I also coordinate with his chartered accountant on his business investments and look after the financial aspects and up keep of the farmhouse and botanical laboratory."

"You are doing a lot of different activities which seem to me very interesting. Moreover, you are so close to a creative person of repute. I met him twice but did not know so much about him. For how long you have worked here?"

"For the last seven to eight years. My uncle worked here before me.""Who stays at the farmhouse?"

"Mr. Nath, Madam Gayatri Devi, Mr. Karan, who is madam's grandson, and me. Then there are staff members who live in the staff quarters. Karan has gone to Mumbai for about three to four weeks."

"Oh, then I will not be able to meet him."

"Why?"

"I am here, for two weeks only. Where is Green Park? I am to appear for the interview there."

"We have already passed that area. It is not too far from the farmhouse."

The journey from the station took about an hour, as there was a lot of traffic. It was still daylight when they reached the farmhouse. Gayatri Devi and Premnath were waiting for Archana. As soon as she came up to them, Gayatri hugged her with affection and kissed her on the forehead. She shook hands with Premnath who also kissed her on the forehead. Then Gayatri said,"Well, dear, do you want a cup of tea or do you want to freshen up first?"

"I'd like some tea first. It's so cold."

Gayatri instructed Shobha accordingly. She started asking about her friend Savitri. Tea and snacks were served, and Archana and Vinod had a cup of tea. Gayatri next asked, "When and where is your interview? Savitri told me that you have come for an interview."

"Yes Aunty, I have an interview on Monday at Green Park. There is still time for that." While drinking tea, Archana told them about her interview and the possibility of her aunt coming to Delhi to stay with her in case she would get the job. Gayatri expressed great enthusiasm over the prospect of her old friend staying in Delhi. It started getting colder, so they went inside. Gayatri Devi went upstairs with Archana to show her the bedroom she would occupy. The room was next to Karan's bedroom, just above Vinod's room.

The next morning Archana got up quite early and went out into the garden for a walk. She saw Premnath talking to someone. She thought that the person standing with Premnath was probably the gardener as he had some gardening tool in his hand. She went up to them and wished Premnath good morning and got an equally warm response. She made an excuse and continued her walk to the other side of the garden. When she completed two rounds on the paved pathway, she saw Vinod coming towards her. "Good morning, Miss. How do you like the place?"

"A very good morning to you too. I like the place very much. It is beyond my imagination. Why do you call me Miss? Please call me Archana. I think I am younger than you." Archana said the last sentence smiling.

"Surely you must be younger than me, I am thirty-two years old."

"Sure, I am about four years younger."

Vinod changed the topic from age to the garden and said, "Everyone who comes here likes the garden. My boss is the brain behind this beautiful garden and landscaping. He is a master in this art."

"After looking around I can easily say that such a fabulous scene can only be created by a master."

"The Municipal Corporation of Delhi has built a park nearby for which Mr. Nath was the consultant. The park is on a large area of land and is worth a visit."

Archana said excitedly, "I would love to visit the place. Will you take me there? I shall talk to aunty. She may even like to accompany us."

"I think you better talk to Madam. As far as I am concerned, I will happily take you there." Although Vinod called Gayatri Devi grandma on her insistence, he always referred to her as a madam.

Vinod continued, "You may also like to see some historical monuments in Delhi. Madam told me that you write poetry."

Archana replied a bit shyly, "I try my hand at poetry sometimes. And I like natural surroundings more than shopping centers or markets. I would like to visit some historical monuments."

"Delhi is full of historical sites."

"My aunt suggested I see places like Qutub Minar, Jama Masjid, India Gate, Red Fort, and Purana Quila. When I had visited her earlier in Delhi, I only saw markets like Connaught Place, Karol Bagh, etc., or went to the movies. Now my tastes have been changed."

"Whenever I am free from my work I am at your disposal. Only you haveto talk to Madam first." They said goodbye to each other and went their separate ways.

Premnath, Gayatri, and Archana were at the breakfast table when Premasked Gayatri, "Has Vinod eaten his breakfast?"

"Yes, he has, he was telling me that after completing some paper work he will be going to the library in search of some book you wanted."

"Yes, but now another book has come to my mind which he can buy from the market."

Archana observed that both uncle and aunt started eating their breakfast.

She found it an appropriate time to talk about what was on her mind. "Should we go to see some historical places? Savitri Aunty asked me not to miss the Qutub Minar, India Gate, and a few other places."

"I would surely like to go with you to see these places, but I feel a bit feverish, and it is quite cold outside. I will speak to Vinod to take you to see some of these places."

Archana said in reply, "Aunty I will stay with you to take care of you if you are not well."

"Oh, I am not in such bad shape that I need someone to take care of me."

Premnath proposed, "It will be better if we ask Vinod to take Archana. They can go to the book shop and library to collect my books and can then visit the other places. I don't need the books till the evening."

When they were in the car, Archana said to Vinod, "Please also show me Green Park if we pass it."

"We will be passing it."

Vinod asked the driver to take the car to the Kutub Minar. There was a huge garden around the Minar and a big restaurant. Archana and Vinod went up to the Minar. It was enchanting and awesome. The sun had come out, but the weather was still quite cool. As they were wandering around a scene from an old Hindi movie *Tere Ghar Ke Samne* flashed through Vinod's mind, in which Dev Anand and Nutan were singing a love song on the Kutub Minar staircase. He started humming the song unconsciously, smiling while doing so. Then an idea stuck with him, and he asked her, "May I ask you a personal question?"

"You may."

"When you are so well settled in Lucknow as a school teacher why did you apply for a job here?"

"Oh, I thought your question would be more personal! I wanted a change.

This job looked exciting. I always wanted to be more involved in literary activities. I am hoping that an editorial job will give me the opportunity." She smiled and Vinod smiled back.

It was Archana's turn to ask a personal question, but she did not bother to take his permission. "How do you like your job as private secretary to Nath Uncle?"

"It is a great privilege to be so close to a personality like Mr. Nath. He is not only a person of extraordinary talents but a very decent human being as well. I have learned a lot from him in the last eight years." They came near the restaurant, so Vinod proposed, "Let's go inside. We can continue our discussion while enjoying a cup of coffee."

"Good idea!"

Vinod placed the order with Archana's consent. She was still thinking about Vinod's reply. "Have you any hobbies other than your job?"

"Yes, I like reading and reciting Urdu poetry, but I can't read Urdu so I read the *shairis* and *ghazals* in Devnagari script."

"That's interesting. I would like to hear you reciting Urdu poetry. Howdid you get interested in it?"

"I am a graduate of Lucknow University, so it was natural to get interested in Urdu poetry. All our cultural programs were full of Urdu poetry recitations." While taking a sip of coffee Archana, agreeing with Vinod, said, "I was also a student there, although a few years previous than you. I know the impact of Urdu there."

"Karan speaks very highly of the language."

"What does he say?"

"He says Urdu is the language of lovers. The broken hearts get cured by simply listening to Urdu poetry."

"It's so true!"

Vinod agreed, "I like Karan's views because they are impartial. He says Urdu is a hundred percent an Indian language. It was developed in India and although it is written in the Perso-Arabic script much of its syntax and vocabulary were borrowed from the Hindi-Sanskrit derivatives of Northern India. That's why it's so like Hindi when spoken."

"Karan's views are excellent and so is your way of expressing them."

"You know Karan is seven to eight years younger than me and comes tome sometimes for advice, but he is so mature that I sometimes feel I am learning from him."

Both remained silent for a few moments then Vinod enquired, "What are your other hobbies?"

"Well, reading detective novels like Sherlock Holmes and Perry Mason."

"That's interesting. I read a lot of Hindi detective novels when I was in high school, but I can't compare myself with you as I am not capable of writing poetry like you."

"How can you say that? I just write for a local paper and a few Hindi magazines."

"In which magazines do you write?" "Kadambani, Sarita, Mukta, Vaneeta, etc."

"That means you are writing poetry of a high standard. All these magazines are very reputed. I sometimes see Madam reading them."

Archana gave a smile and said, "You seem to have a habit of appreciating others."

They left the restaurant and Vinod took her to the 7-metre high iron pillar in the Kutub premises, which was made in the 4th century during Gupta's period. He told her that it stood in the open in all weather conditions without any sign of rusting!

They went to the car and Vinod asked the driver to go towards Green Park. He bought the book Premnath had asked for from the market and then taking the address for the interview from Archana he showed her the place where she had to go on Monday. Since it was time for lunch, they ate in a small restaurant in the market. Vinod gave the driver some money to have his lunch. After lunch, they went to India Gate.

Archana liked the Lutyens' bungalows on both sides of the tree-lined, wide roads on the way to India Gate. Vinod explained that the area was a remarkable example of urban town planning that had not lost its relevance even today. Looking at the vast spaces between the Rashtrapati Bhawan and the India Gate she became poetic. They choose a spot on the lawns where there was enough sunshine and sat down.

Archana could not resist saying, "It's all so wonderful, and the area looks like an archaeological site. Such heritage needs to be well maintained for posterity."

Vinod smiled, "Some people are against these structures as they remind usof our colonial past."

Archana protested, "What! Can we run from our past? If something is good even if it is a product of colonial past it should be allowed to flourish."

Vinod agreed.

After enjoying the sunshine for about an hour Vinod said, "We have to get books from the British Library. We better move."

They got up and moved towards the car. On reaching the farmhouse, Vinod went to the office below the laboratory to hand over the books to Premnath while Archana on discovering that Gayatri Devi was in her bedroom went to her to inquire about her health. Gayatri had a mild fever, but she asked her guest how she had spent her day. She was pleased that Archana was in a happy mood after her first day in Delhi.

When both were in beds in their respective rooms, Archana and Vinod were thinking about each other. Vinod appeared a thorough gentleman to her. She thought of him as a qualified, mild-mannered person with an interest in Urdu poetry and who was cracking jokes at the right time. The chief quality that appealed to her was his appreciation of others. His handling of the fair sex with acute sensitivity also impressed her. Vinod was impressed by Archana; her simplicity, natural beauty, original thinking, and above all her poetic nature.

Both had a problem choosing their life partners. Whenever he went to his parents near Lucknow for a visit, he was pressurized more and more to get married. He even agreed to see a few girls. Gayatri Devi showed him a few girls also, but none had appealed to him as a wife. Today was perhaps the first day in his life that he felt a sudden surge of attraction towards a girl.

Archana's feelings were almost similar. Her reason for refusing to marry was a little different. Her best friend

Mahima, who was doing the M.A. course with her fell in love with a man. One day, to Archana's horror her friend attempted suicide because the man she loved got engaged to another girl from a rich family. Mahima's life was saved due to the timely detection of her suicide attempt but the incident put a scar on Archana's delicate mind. A few months later, there was another incident in her neighborhood. A girl living in the house opposite her aunt after a month of marriage returned to her parents because they could not fulfill the greedy demands of her in-laws and her husband. These two incidents created a feeling of revulsion in her towards men in general. She decided she would marry only if she found an appropriate person, otherwise, she would prefer to stay single like her aunt.

That night she felt that her wait was over.

CHAPTER 24

Archana woke up refreshed in the morning. She went out for a walk andmet Premnath again with his gardener on the front lawns. Archana wished him good morning. After responding he said, "How would you like to pass the day today?"

"Vinod told me about the park which was made under your direction. Will you be able to show it to me today?"

"I am very sorry today I have to visit a friend who has come from Mumbai and will be leaving for Vaisnu Devi tomorrow."

"Oh, I see. Gayatri Aunty is also not well enough to take me there."

"Let me see. Why don't you go with Vinod? I can ask him to postpone his other work until the evening."

"I have no problem if you allow him to accompany me to the park."

With a sigh of relief, Premnath said, "I will ask him. You better take a packed lunch with you. I hope you will enjoy it there." Thanking Premnath for his consideration, she carried on with her morning walk. She did not see Vinod anywhere in the garden and sat for some time near the pond where the morning sun was just coming out. She was in high spirits but the person who raised them was not visible. She got up and went to Gayatri Devi's room to enquire about her health. She seemed better, sitting on a chair reading a magazine.

Archana looking at her said, "My dear Aunty, how are you today? You seem well. Thank God! Are you all, right? Let's go out today."

Gayatri while putting the magazine aside smiled at her and replied, "Well dear I am better, but I still have a mild temperature. Today is the third day I hope to recover completely by tomorrow. Make your plans with Vinod today. Your uncle also must visit a friend. For tomorrow I promise to accompany you to wherever you want to go."

Archana promptly replied, "Yes Aunty I know uncle is busy. He told me when I was out in the garden for my morning walk. I asked him to accompany me to the park nearby, and he suggested that I may go with Vinod."

Gayatri said happily, "Yes do go to the park. It is worth seeing. You will see your uncle's contributions there. Moreover, such an open space may not suit me for a few days. Your uncle's suggestion that you go with Vinod is very appropriate. He is like a family member."

Archana had no objections to visiting the park with Vinod. That was what she wanted. She could also understand Premnath and Gayatri Devi's dilemma that they were not able to entertain their guest themselves. Gayatri started asking her again about her friend and Lucknow, and then suddenly asked, "Dear, why you have not married? If you don't mind, I can show you a few boys who match your age and talents."

Archana felt it necessary to clarify the matter, so she said, "Aunty I am not saying that I will not marry like Savitri Aunty.

When I find a person of my choice, I will inform you first that is my promise."

 On this pleasant note, the talk ended. At the breakfast table, Premnath asked Vinod to take Archana to Swadeshi Park. Vinod who was more than happy to have Archana's company said in a normal tone, "As you wish Sir."

Archana said, "I have seen a motorbike in the garage. Can we go on the bike?"

Vinod replied, "It's Karan's bike. I will have to look for the key."

Gayatri said, "Karan gave me the key. It is in my room. Take some foodfor lunch. It's enjoyable to eat out there." And the program was settled.

Archana and Vinod were driving down the highway on the bike towards Swadeshi Park with a packed lunch and unpacked emotions. Vinod took the bike to the parking lot, picked up the food packets, and after taking entry tickets, they went ahead to the park. They had also brought a mat. After moving around for about fifteen minutes, they selected a spot where they could sit. Archana was looking around like a child seeing the world for the first time. Vinod could well gauge that her amazement was in proportion to the highly creative imagination with which the park was developed. All around her were beautiful flowers and trees on the natural-looking landscaped grounds, so well planted that it dumb founded her. Vinod said, "You have seen only a fragment of the complete concept. I can understand your emotional response."

Archana took a deep breath and said, "It's so wonderful. Can we make our surroundings so beautiful that it forces us to make an observation as a part ofour indulgence? Then one may have to do a lot of efforts to find out the rare introverts."

"You are not only a poet but a psychologist also."

"Oh, it is neither poetry nor psychology but a reality in front of us."

They were silent for a while, to cope with their emotions. These beautiful natural surroundings always created emotions in people, but in this case, it was different. They were not just ordinary people; they had an interest in poetry. When two young hearts start liking each other, they move to a different plane and such venues give a further boost to their feelings.

However, since Vinod and Archana belonged to a mature age group, everything was within the norms.

Archana said, "I never thought that something so important would happen in my life while I am in Delhi."

"May I know what that is?" "It's very difficult to say."

"Please try to tell me if you think I am worthy to hear it."

Archana was uncertain how to put it, but Vinod's words made her put aside her inhibitions, so she said, "This morning Aunty was asking me why I have not got married?"

"What did you say?" Vinod asked eagerly

Archana smiled and said, "I replied in the same way I replied to you and made a promise."

"What was that?" Vinod's eagerness was easily noticeable.

"I promised her that she would be the first person I would tell if I start liking someone."

"Is there any chance of your telling her in the near future?"

"Perhaps."

Their conversation ended when their eyes met. Their next communication was through their eyes only.

Vinod was determined not to express his feelings until Archana opened her heart. Now time seemed to pass slower and slower. For both of them, the next few moments felt like a few hours, Archana ultimately said, "NowI have to tell Aunty about the boy I have started liking."

"Who is the lucky guy?" Vinod's anxiety was at its extreme.

"It's you," Archana said, lowering her face shyly after declaring her love so boldly. Vinod, who had sensed Archana's inclination toward him, was still totally dumbfounded at her unexpected words. After he was able to digest what he heard, he said, "Then I shall have to tell my parents also."

"What do you want to tell your parents?"

"Very simple, that I have found the girl who will be my life partner."

Both of them laughed and Archana came closer to him. They sat for a few minutes in the same position without moving. Vinod then asked, "May I bring something for you to drink?"

"As you please". Vinod knew where to get cold drinks and returned in ten minutes with two cans of fruit juice.

Archana, with a smile on her face, started the conversation again. She said, "When will you inform your parents about your life partner?"

"Only when, grandma, my boss, and your parents approve our relationship." Vinod referred to Gayatri Devi as grandma for the first time in front of Archana. She found nothing wrong with his logic. Looking at his watch he said, "Let us see some more of the park before we take lunch." They got up with their baggage, and Vinod taking the lead moved on.

Beautiful multicolored flowers on the huge grassy landscape had a soothing effect on their charged emotions. After a good walk, they felt more at peace and self-assured. Archana selected the site for lunch. They ate their lunch and then had a cup of tea, which was brought in a flask. They rested for a while and then moved on to the unexplored areas of the park.

Archana was quite overwhelmed emotionally by her own expression, but despite that, she could not resist openly expressing her joy at what she saw. Vinod had seen the park several times earlier and was engrossed in his thoughts. He merely nodded his head in reply to Archana's expressions of joy. One thought that repeatedly disturbed him was that in the Indian context, Archana's aunt and parents might not approve of him as their son-in-law as he worked at Nath's. This thought remained with him, even though he knew he got a good salary and was well respected by all. As far as Gayatri Devi and

Premnath were concerned, he was sure that the news of his marrying would give them immense pleasure. Premnath's dependence on him, so that he himself could indulge completely in his creative work, was well known. Vinod perhaps did not know his own reputation as an honest, upright person, who was widely acknowledged amongst Premnath's friends and relations, and which was a rare quality to find these days.

Vinod was in a doubtful state so he said, "I doubt if your aunt and parents will agree to our relationship."

"Why do you think so?"

"Well, I belong to a different caste. They may even think my job is not that secure."

"Expel all these doubts from your mind." "Are my doubts baseless?"

Archana then tried to explain to him, "No comments on your doubts. I only know my parents are desperate for me to get married. They keep reminding me that they are old and will not remain with me for long. I had to keep them well assured that one day I will marry a person of my choice which keeps their emotions under check," She concluded by saying, "I am sure now they will jump with joy and respond happily."

As Archana was reassuring Vinod, they reached the farmhouse.

CHAPTER-25

Karan remained busy all day and even up to late nights. When he got the initial details of the project, he estimated it would take more than a month to complete it in the normal course. It became a challenge for him to complete it at the earliest possible time, preferably within three weeks. He did not want to leave Reena alone at such a crucial juncture and wanted to be at her side, so he was working day and night. Every technical detail was at his fingertips because he had done a similar project for another client in Delhi only a few months ago. He only had to proceed with the project, according to the client's specifications. He even worked on Saturday. Only Sunday was free for him, so he used it to wander around Mumbai.

After dinner, while he was watching the news on the television in his room, his phone rang. It was Reena, and she informed him about the latest developments, "The reply from the young man who saw me was negative." She continued further telling him that he clearly told his parents that he was not ready to marry for the time being, though he told them that he did like her. Reena's uncle was very upset with the message which he had received from his friend only that very day, but at the same time, he did not know the effect of such a wonderful message on herself and her parents who were very happy with the news. She then explained that her father would talk to her uncle at the first possible opportunity within the next few days.

The news did not have any positive effect on Karan as he already knew the boy's mind in his previous talk with Reena. He wanted to know Reena's parents' final reply after their talk with her uncle, so he remained in a sober mood. He decided to go out to the seaside.

The weather in Mumbai at that hour was excellent. Mumbai city came alive during these hours because all day everyone is busy with work. His guest house was quite near the sea, so he decided to go there. There were a lot of people around. He found a comparatively isolated place and sat down. The sodium light, a few yards away, was illuminating a huge area. He observed the waves, which looked like a serpent moving. Then he turned his eyes towards the horizon. A passer by would have got the impression that he was observing nature or thinking about his beloved or creating a few poetic stanzas, but in fact, none of these things were in his thoughts. He was brooding on human nature. How much human nature was different from physical nature even when it was the product of physical nature? His thought process went further, and he asked himself, "How do thoughts and emotions make all this difference? How does this element, which is called consciousness and can also be termed psychological or spiritual, enters physical nature? Even when it remains in physical existence, it remains so aloof! Not only this, these thoughts and emotions may or may not be part of consciousness but make a lot of difference between one person to another." The chain of his thoughts was suddenly broken by the noise of the waves, which were rising higher and higher. He moved to a safer place and sat down.

He went further deeper into his thoughts as he felt the urge to think about the natural phenomena for which he could not get any reply. He often thought the same and was once again engrossed in it that night. One thought that made him shiver a few times was, "When and why did time start and when will it end? One reply to this question, propounded by the ancient Indian philosophers and modern scientific thinkers, is that there is no start or end to time. Time is infinite, but he could never visualize the concept of infinite time. It remained unthinkable also for him to think of even finite time. He yearned to know the truth. "Does the reality, as it exists, differs from what the human mind perceives?" Karan just got a flash, but as usual, could not see any clear solution. The most satisfactory reply that came to his mind was that nobody knew it. He started thinking, "Perhaps the human mind is not developed yet enough to visualize it." He came out of his thinking spell by taking a few deep breaths and then did some brisk walking. It resulted in calming down his mind and he felt peaceful.

CHAPTER 26

After spending a memorable day at Swadeshi Park, Archana thought of meeting Gayatri Devi in her room but to her satisfaction, she found her up and about. She was sitting in the drawing room on a sofa reading Femina magazine. Gayatri kissed Archana on the forehead and asked her if she had enjoyed her visit to the park. Vinod, who had accompanied her slipped away with some excuse when Archana went toward Gayatri Devi. Premnath entered the hall, inched towards the two ladies, and asked Archana, "How did you like the place?"

"Uncle, you have created a dreamland." "In short you liked it."

"It was beyond words."

Premnath smiled and sat down. Gayatri gave instructions to Sheru to bring tea and to send also to Vinod's room. Then she proposed the next day's program, "Shall we go to Dilli Haat tomorrow? You will enjoy the place."

"Oh, my dear Aunty, you are taking so much care of me even for one day you don't want me to remain in the house fearing I may get bored."

Gayatri smiled at her and Premnath said, "Then I will also accompany both of you as I like the place very much. They have developed the place while keeping its natural surroundings intact."

Archana gave her reaction to him "Uncle you have made me curious about the place.

After tea, Premnath took Archana to the library. She admired its size with the display of so many books and the seating arrangement so that one could enjoy reading in front of the huge windows facing the beautiful garden outside.

After getting up in the morning Archana went for a walk and found Vinod already exercising. They met with a smile and moved to the pool side selecting a spot where the sun was shining and sat down. Vinod asked her eagerly, "Have you told grandma?"

"Not yet."

"When do you plan to tell her?"

"I will be telling her most probably on Monday after my interview." "Is there any link?"

"I think so but I will explain it afterwards if there is any need."

"It's all right. Let me move now. I want to meet you only in their presence."

"As you consider fit. Today I am going to Dilli Haat with uncle and aunty."

"Have a good day." Vinod smiled and went towards the main building. Archana thought that Vinod did not want to take any risk until the matter was clear. She continued sitting there for about half an hour and then went to her room to get ready.

Dilli Haat was a huge place where Indian arts and crafts were on display for sale. All Indian states were represented there. There was a big food bazaar where one could get food specialties from several states at very reasonable prices. The seating arrangement for all the food stalls was common. There were grassy lawns where one could sit and relax, and the ambiance was serene. Premnath and Gayatri bought a few decoration pieces. Archana was very happy to see the latest and good quality Indian arts and crafts in one place. The place was crowded as people moved from one shop to another. They ate lunch and moved around for some more time, but one day was not enough to explore the whole area properly. On the way back they stopped at the INA market as Gayatri wanted to buy a few gifts for Archana, her parents, and Savitri Devi.

When the car was moving toward the farmhouse Gayatri asked Archana, "Your interview is on Monday. Do you want to make any preparations for that?"

"No aunty, there is no need for preparations." "Then we can go tomorrow to Ashok Vihar." "Yes, we can go."

Gayatri asked Premnath, "Do you want to accompany us tomorrow?" "No. Tomorrow I want to work on my book."

"I think Vinod can accompany Archana to the interview on Monday." "I will ask Vinod to coordinate with her."

Archana without saying anything welcomed the decision of the elders.

Their discussion made her more determined to tell Gayatri Devi about Vinod only after her interview.

At dinner, though Vinod was present, neither Archana nor Vinod showed any sign that indicated any kind of mutual development between them.

Premnath gave Vinod the good news that he would be accompanying Archana for the interview and to fix the program according to her schedule. Vinod replied that he would fix it during the morning walk.

Archana and Vinod were thinking about each other when they were in bed. Both were in a strange state of mind because they had taken such an important decision of their lives.

During their morning walk, Archana and Vinod met and shook hands, as they were in a place where they could be seen. Vinod showed more confidence on this occasion. He suggested to Archana, "Let's move to a quiet spot." And he led her to the Lover's Point and took her hand in his and said, "What is the time of the interview?"

"11 a.m."

"Then we must leave latest by 10 a.m." "It's better to reach early in such cases."

"No problem, we can start at 9.30 in the morning." "All right that's final. Can someone see us here?"

"Nobody can, and we are here to fix the program which is known to the elders."

"That's why you look so confident today, sitting so close to me."

"Oh, you think we are sitting so close? Then you have no idea of closeness."

Vinod said it jokingly, but Archana was not ready to accept defeat so easily. She said, "Show me your definition of closeness." Vinod took her in his arms. His chest was just touching her breast. The pressure between them increased and Vinod put his lips on hers. They remained in that position for about two minutes, when Vinod removed his lips from her and loosened his grip; Archana's face was flushed, and she said, "If someone sees us now?"

"Don't worry, I was quite aware of the whole situation, but I must say, it is the first wonderful experience of my life.

"Should we not observe some limits?"

"We are very well within our limits, but I may not repeat it until we get engaged."

"That's a good idea."

They got up to go and Archana told him that she was going to Ashok Vihar with Gayatri Devi.

When the four of them were around the table at dinner, Premnath asked his sister, "How is everyone at Ashok Vihar?"

"They are fine. Everyone was asking about you. Even Vinnie and Ishu were asking me why we did not bring granduncle."

"All right, the next time you go I will accompany you."

Premnath then asked Vinod, "Have you fixed up with Archana for her interview?"

"Yes Sir, we have decided about the program."

Addressing his sister he asked, "Is there any message from Karan?"

"He called yesterday when you were busy with the gardener. He is well and asked about you."

"Is there any progress about him?" Gayatri understood what he meant and replied, "He says any further development will be possible only when he comes back."

"I really like the girl Reena and wish her to be Karan's wife." Gayatri smiled and said, "If God is willing that will definitely happen."

Vinod and Archana started from the farmhouse at a mutually fixed time with Sohan Lal at the wheel. Vinod told him where to go, and then turning towards Archana asked, "Are you well prepared for the interview?"

"As such, there is no preparation for these types of interviews."

Vinod changed the topic and said, "You have not spoken to grandma about us as yet?"

"No, not yet I will talk to her today if time permits. I feel a bit nervous."

"I also feel nervous, but as promised I am to inform her first." "I hope and wish God helps us."

They reached the place of the interview at about ten thirty. The publisher's building was an independent five-storied building. Vinod went inside with Archana to the reception where a young lady met them and asked them to sit down. After about ten minutes, another young lady entered and called out Archana's name. She then gave Archana a form to fill. She also gave the same form to another man who had entered after

Archana. The form had four pages, which Archana completed in about fifteen minutes. The same lady came after another twenty minutes and collected the forms from both the candidates.

Vinod looked at his watch. It was more than fifty minutes since Archana went in for the interview. He became busy with his thoughts about her.

When again after some time he found no signs of her, he picked up a magazine from the table and started turning its pages. When she finally returned, Vinod looked at his watch and calculated that the interview took one-and-a-half hours. Archana looked happy and informed him that it was a good experience and that they would send the result within two days. "I gave them the address and telephone numbers of the farmhouse."

As they went toward the car, Vinod asked her, "Now what's your program?"

"Well, Baba I am in your city. It is up to you to tell me if there is any program..."

"Ok then let's have lunch here in the market after which we can decide about our program."

"Well, I don't mind," Archana said, smiling. Vinod instructed the driver to go to the same restaurant where they had gone earlier. He gave Sohan Lal some money for his lunch and stepped out of the car with Archana. As both were in a relaxed mood, they walked leisurely and found a table near the window from where they could see an enchanting, tiny park beyond the veranda and road. Vinod started the conversation, "Today may be our last day of freedom if you speak to grandma."

"I understand but talking to her is important to mobilize the matter further."

Vinod agreed. Then they decided to go to Lodhi Gardens. They roamed around Lodhi Gardens holding hands. Archana liked the garden but could not help comparing it with Swadeshi Park and said, "It's really very beautiful with the monuments in the background but it can't be compared with the fabulous park we have seen three days ago. They found a few isolated places shaded by trees and surrounded by bushes. They embraced and kissed each other. They enjoyed the place for about two hours and then decided to go back.

Vinod asked her, "If you are selected for the job when will you join."

"They asked me that in the interview. My reply was that I could join immediately after the school examinations are over, preferably at the beginning of April. They had no objection to that." Archana continued, "They asked if I had any editorial experience. I show them a few volumes of my school magazine where I was editor of the Hindi section. From their expression, I could make out that they liked the magazines very much."

"That's a good sign."

Vinod again reminded her to talk to grandma that evening positively and to let him know about the outcome at the earliest possible after her talk with her.

As soon as Archana entered the drawing room Gayatri and Premnath greeted her and asked about her interview, "The interview went well. They will inform me in two days. I gave them the address and telephone numbers of the farmhouse."

"I think you will be selected," Premnath said. Gayatri ordered tea, which was served in about ten minutes, while Premnath and Archana cracked jokes with each other. Vinod kept smiling during the entire period. After tea, Premnath said something to Vinod in a low tone and they went to the office. Archana then said, "Aunty let us sit in your room as I want to talk with you about something very important." Gayatri immediately got up and they went to her room. They sat there on easy chairs side by side and Gayatri said with curiosity,

"What's the matter, dear? Please tell me."

"Aunty I promised you a few days back that you will be the first person to whom I would inform when I select a person as my life partner."

Gayatri Devi could not believe what she heard and cried out, "Oh, my God! Have you found someone? Tell me without delay please."

Archana was trying to find the right words to talk about something so momentous in her life. She gathered her courage and said, "My dear Aunty the life partner I have selected is very well known to you. He is uncle's private secretary, Vinod."

"Oh!" Gayatri's mouth was opened in amazement for a few seconds. When she could speak, she said, "I just can't believe my ears!" Then suddenly she came alive and hugged Archana closely and kissed her forehead several times. She expressed her happiness saying, "I am really very happy. Vinod is a good person, but he was not ready, a bit resistant to such things. You were also like him." She said the last words laughing loudly.

Archana then decided to get a clearer view, "Aunty, do you have any objection? Please tell me if you have. We are both clear that we will give up the relationship if you and uncle will not like it."

"No! No! I don't have any objections. On the contrary, I am very happy to hear this."

"Thank God at least you approve it. Now the whole matter rests on Uncle's consent."

"I think Premnath will also be very happy to hear this. The only matter that may become an issue is that he is a Brahmin, and you are an Arora (an off-shoot of the Kshatriya caste). I hope there will be no objection from your parents on this count."

"If there is any objection on this count then I will never marry."

"I hope things will be settled in an amicable manner. After consulting Premnath, I will talk to Savitri. Should I call her here?"

"If she comes within two to three days then we can both go back according to my schedule."

"What is the hurry to go back?"

"Aunty you don't know how I managed to get such a long leave in January. I completed the syllabus and arranged for my colleague, a close friend of mine, to take my classes along with hers and also to take extra classes if there is any need."

"I understand school pressure during these days. Let me inform her after talking to Premnath without any loss of time."

She went out of her room asking Archana to wait for her there. She saw the light on in Premnath's bedroom, which meant he was there, so she went inside and found Premnath reading some papers. She said, "I have come to give you good news."

"What is it? Does it concern Karan?" "No. Not Karan but Archana and Vinod."

Premnath put the papers on one side of the table and asked his sister to sit down and tell him everything. Gayatri said, "Archana and Vinod have started liking each other." Not expecting such exciting news at this late hour, but not sure if the news was correct, he said, "Who gave you this information?"

"Archana herself told me."

"If that is so, it's fantastic news."

Both Premnath and Gayatri Devi had been trying to convince Vinod for the last three to four years to get married but without any result. Gayatri Devi even showed him a few girls during that period, but nothing matured. Both the brother and sister discussed all the possible aspects and then decided to call Vinod to get first-hand information from him.

When Vinod arrived, he told them that he loved Archana and wanted to make her his wife. He also explained to them that Archana had responded, but they decided to go ahead only if Premnath and Gayatri Devi would be accepting the relationship whole heartedly, otherwise they would try to remain just friends, however hard it may be. Vinod's explanation satisfied both and they congratulated him.

Then Premnath said, "I hope parents on both sides agree."

Vinod replied promptly, "Sir my parents are not going to object, not on the matter of caste differences. On the contrary, they will be overjoyed that I have found my life partner."

Premnath then suggested Gayatri Devi talk to her friend Savitri on the telephone without delay. Gayatri Devi went to her room and told Archana what had been discussed. Archana also wanted the two friends to discuss the matter.

Gayatri, without wasting time, called her friend in Lucknow and appraised her of the situation along with Premnath's and her views on the affair. She requested her friend to come to Delhi after consulting Archana's parents, to finalize the man for her niece.

At dinner, even though both Archana and Vinod were present they did not talk to each other. They joined the conversation of the elders. In her bed, at night Archana's head was full of dreams and there was no sign of sleep. She was amazed that for so many years she had avoided the subject of marriage and suddenly Vinod and her marriage were the only two things that filled her mind. Vinod's situation was almost similar. He was dreaming of the time when all factors would favor his marriage to Archana.

The next evening Gayatri Devi received a phone call from Lucknow.

Savitri Devi said that she would be coming to Delhi the next day by the Shatabadi Express. She also said that she had discussed the matter with Archana's parents. They had no objection if their daughter was willing and Premnath and Gayatri approved of the relationship. Gayatri noted down her coach and seat numbers and the exact time of arrival of the train.

Archana woke up early. After refreshing herself, she came out for her walk. On her first round, no one was visible. In her second round, she saw a figure approaching her. It was none other than Vinod. Both of them smiled and wished each other and went to their favorite Lover's Point. They sat there comfortably. Vinod said, "I am a bit nervous because your aunt is coming today to select or reject me."

"Don't worry about her. I know her she will only agree with my choice."

"That's a big assurance." They sat for another few minutes in silence, when Vinod suddenly said, "It's better if I go now. Why should we show others at this stage that we have no control in meeting each other?" Archana agreed and the next moment, Vinod disappeared. Archana sat there for some more time. She was in the mood to write some poetry that she was singing, more in her mind than through her lips.

After breakfast, Archana and Gayatri came out to the front lawns.

Premnath and Vinod went to the office. Premnath's book was taking good shape. About a hundred pages had been typed on the computer by an employee hired for this purpose. He had done the typing from Premnath's notebook. His work was thoroughly checked by Vinod, and Premnath received it in the form of a final copy.

Gayatri and Archana were enjoying the pleasant mid-January sunshine and Gayatri was asking Archana about her life in Lucknow. She decided to go with Archana to receive Savitri in the evening at the station. The telephone inside was ringing. Sheru brought the cordless phone and gave it to Gayatri. The call was for Archana, so Gayatri gave it to her. After listening, she gave it back to Sheru and informed Gayatri Devi, "Aunty, they have selected me for the job. I must join on or before the first of April."

"Congratulations! That's very good news. It has now double significance for you as you are to marry and settle down here." Archana accepted her thanks with shyness. Gayatri Devi immediately informed Premnath and Vinod in the office. Both showed happiness and came out to congratulate Archana. She accepted their congratulations and thanked them. Gayatri Devi called Sheru, gave him money, and asked him to bring some sweets. Archana was so overwhelmed by Gayatri's gesture that she hugged her saying, "My dear, sweet aunty!"

When Premnath joked about Archana's double achievements, not only Archana but even Vinod showed signs of shyness, which were clearly reflected on their faces.

On the way to the station, both ladies were so busy talking that they only knew they had arrived when the car stopped in front of the station. They walked to the main entrance and Archana bought two platform tickets and they went to the platform where the train was expected in ten minutes. It was a sight to see the three ladies meet. Within a few minutes, they were in the back seat of the car, with Savitri sandwiched between the other two. Savitri Devi was eager to know all the details in the shortest possible time. Gayatri felt Archana was feeling a bit hesitant and shy to tell her everything, so she took the responsibility and told Savitri all the details from her point of view. Archana seemed satisfied with the way Gayatri Devi explained everything.

Gayatri Devi even told her friend about Vinod's family background. She said that his father was a retired Postmaster with two sons and a daughter. All the other children were married. Vinod's brother was staying with his parents.

Regarding Vinod's job, she informed her friend that he was getting a good salary and was like a family member. Premnath took care to make his job pensionable through insurance cover.

Savitri looked satisfied with what she heard from her friend. When she was told about Archana getting the job she was over joyed by the news.

Their talk was interrupted as they reached the farmhouse. Gayatri asked Archana to take Savitri to her bedroom so that she could freshen up. Inside the room, Savitri said to Archana, "Dear how all this happened so suddenly? I just can't believe my ears. Are you really ready for marriage?"

"My dear Aunty, even I don't believe that all this has happened so suddenly. I think I found the person of my choice, so why delay the matter."

"I wish and hope that I like the boy whom you have chosen. Let me take a few minutes to freshen up." After about half an hour, a message came that tea was ready and the others were waiting in the hall. Savitri and Archana went downstairs and found Gayatri and Premnath waiting for them. Premnath and Savitri Devi knew each other quite well. After the initial pleasantries, Gayatri asked Savitri, "May I call Vinod before the tea is served so that you have a good look at him while having tea."

"Sure, I am eager to meet the concerned person."

Gayatri asked Sheru to call Sharma Sahib as he was popularly called by the staff.

When Vinod entered, he wished everyone in general. Since Savitri Devi was a guest, Gayatri Devi, introduced her and they went to the dining table where tea with snacks was served.

During tea, Savitri asked Vinod a few questions, to which he replied politely. The tea session ended on a pleasant note.

When the three ladies were sitting on the bed in Gayatri's room after tea, Gayatri asked Savitri, "Now tell us frankly what your views about Vinod are."

"I liked him. He is quite fit to be Archana's husband. He looks like a mature, young man. I would like him to talk to his parents without further delay and take their concurrence so that we may go ahead with the formalities." Both the ladies were quite happy to hear this and Archana was in an ecstatic state of mind.

During dinner, Vinod was asked to talk to his parents so that Savitri Devi could leave Delhi with the knowledge of their approval.

That night aunt and niece talked at length about the new affair and Archana's future.

Vinod spoke to his uncle who had worked earlier as Premnath's private secretary. He gave all details of Archana and her family. By chance, Vinod's uncle had met Savitri Devi earlier when he was at the farmhouse. He requested his uncle to confirm the matter in a day or two after talking it over with his parents. Vinod also spoke to his mother and gave her the girl's details and requested her to give her frank opinion about the affair. Vinod's mother was so desperate for her son's marriage that she informed him right there that she was ready to accept any girl of his choice.

Savitri wanted to utilize her time in Delhi to meet her old school colleagues, so the three ladies went to Ashok Vihar and Model Town to meet a few of their old friends. Gayatri also visited her house for a few hours with the other two.

The next day Premnath was sitting with the three ladies on the front lawns after breakfast to enjoy the sunshine as well as the conversation about the old school days between two friends.

In the evening Vinod got the formal consent of his parents through his uncle. His father also spoke to him and was happy that at last, he had decided to get married. Later, his mother, who had already agreed, gave him her best wishes and blessings for his future. Premnath and Gayatri received the news with great pleasure. Savitri Devi thanked God that her visit to Delhi was successful. Archana without showing anything outwardly was beyond joy.

Vinod already knew what his parents' reaction would be, but even then, their expressions of happiness at his selection multiplied his joy.

At Savitri Devi's request, Vinod booked two tickets through the travel agent for Lucknow on the Sunday morning Shatabadi Express.

Saturday was a day of discussion of the ceremonial planning before the marriage. Vinod told Savitri Devi frankly that due to Karan's influence his views about the dowry system were similar to his. He would like a simple ring ceremony and marriage. Both the ceremonies could be performed in Lucknow, as his parents lived just two hours away from there. Savitri Devi suggested Vinod visit his parents and fix the dates for the ceremonies with the mutual consent of both the families so everything was settled on a happy note.

That evening Gayatri Devi got a telephone call from Karan. He informed her that he would be arriving in Delhi next Saturday. He particularly requested his grandmother to meet Reena and inform him if any development had taken place. Gayatri gave his grandson an assurance that she would meet Reena the very next day. Gayatri also gave Karan the news of Vinod and Archana's engagement. Karan was happy to hear that unexpected good news. He conveyed his congratulations to both of them.

On Sunday morning, Vinod went to see Savitri Devi and Archana off at the railway station.

CHAPTER-27

Both the brother and sister were sitting on the front lawns after the departure of their guests. Premnath said, "I am really happy that Archana will stay at the farmhouse after her marriage."

"That's an additional bonus. I wish that Karan and Reena's affair also works out."

"I hope so. There will be a lot of hustle and bustle in the farmhouse, which I love."

"If you had agreed to get married when you returned to India things might have been different."

"You know my first experience was so bitter that I decided never to try a second time."

Gayatri changed the topic and said, "I want to invite Reena and her mother here this evening for tea."

"That's an attractive proposition. Invite Reena from my side also as I want to know what she is doing in her garden."

"I will convey your message."

Premnath got up and said, "I am going to the laboratory."

Gayatri dialed Reena's number and said, "I am Gayatri Devi from Nath's, may I know who is speaking?"

"Good morning Aunty I am Rakhi.

"Oh! very good morning to you. How are you?"

"I am fine, thank you. It's been a long time since I heard from you." "I had guests from Lucknow, and they just left today.

I am very sorry I could not talk to you earlier. In fact, I want to invite you all here for tea this evening. My brother is also anxious to meet all of you."

"Aunty, Reena's papa is on a business trip to Singapore with his brother. They will be back tonight." Gayatri paused for a few seconds then said, "Is Reena there?"

"I will call her please hold on."

When Reena came on the line, a lot of pleasantries were exchanged and finally, Gayatri came to the point, "Dear, Karan has told me everything about you before leaving for Mumbai. I really wanted to talk to you personally.

There were guests here from Lucknow who left today. Premnath also asked me to invite you as he wanted to know what changes you have made to your garden."

"Grandma let me speak to my mother. I shall call you in a few minutes."

Reena was a bit puzzled. Had Karan not got a clear picture from her? And was that the reason he wanted his grandmother to meet her? Her uncle did not express his views clearly when her father spoke to him the day before leaving for Singapore. Both Reena and Rakhi stressed Subhash Mukherji to get a clear decision from his elder brother and if necessary to convince him about Karan – his good qualification, a good job with an MNC, and above all his determination not to accept dowry. Subhash Mukherji assured both the ladies that he would spare no efforts regarding the matter of such urgent nature.

Reena was now thinking about Gayatri Devi's invitation. She herself was eager to know Karan's family's views about their affair. Although she was sure that their response was in the affirmative, she was desperate to hear a few soothing words from Karan's grandmother. She got her mother's permission and told Gayatri Devi that she would be coming with her maid in the evening.

Reena was again engrossed in her thoughts. She was a bit worried. She could not explain to Karan that due to her uncle's vague reply there was no conclusion. She called Karan three times during the last two weeks and spoke to him twice. She was ready to take drastic steps even if she would get the support of Karan's family.

Gayatri Devi and Premnath were waiting for her and she was well in time with her maid. After the initial pleasantries, Premnath asked Reena, "What have you done in your garden?"

Reena gave the details about the changes she was contemplating about thelandscaping and new plants, etc. Premnath was quite pleased that she was doing so much in such a short time. Tea and snacks were served and after sitting for about half an hour Premnath excused himself, saying he had somework with Vinod.

On hearing Vinod's name Gayatri suddenly remembered his engagement and told Reena about it. Reena expressed her happiness about such a good development. Then Gayatri came to the main point. "All of us, my brother, Karan's parents, and I are very happy to hear that you both like each other."

Reena kept silent, Gayatri continued, "I liked you from the day I met you and I have no problem saying so, but I want to know your parent's response."

Reena replied, "My parents are very happy to accept my relationship. They both like and appreciate Karan, but due to certain obligations which Karan knows about, my father will be able to give his consent only after getting the green signal from his elder brother." Reena stopped for some time and continued, "At present, my father and uncle are in Singapore. I hope they might have discussed this matter and reached some conclusion. We may know about it by tomorrow."

"I see." Gayatri said after a pause, "Dear if you feel there is any need for me or for my brother to speak to your parents or uncle, please don't hesitate to say so. We both have absolutely no problems talking to anyone on this matter so that everything can be settled at the earliest possible."

Gayatri's words gave Reena strength, "Grandma if there is any need for you to talk to my family, I will inform you. I am very happy to hear that you are so keen to help."

"How can you say this? Karan is my dearest grandson and you will be my dearest grandson's wife." She then hugged Reena and kissed her twice.

Reena told her mother that Karan's grandmother was anxious to see that the matter would get settled at an early date. They were waiting anxiously for Subhash Mukherji's arrival. He called from the airport to say that he had eaten on the flight and subsequently both brothers reached their side of the farmhouse at about 11 p.m. It was cold, so hot coffee was prepared. Rakhi asked her husband initially about his health, business trip, and things of general interest. Then Rakhi came to the main point. She was as desperate as her daughter, due to Reena's tension, wanted a positive outcome as soon as possible. She said, "Have you talked with *Dada* about Reena and Karan?" Subhash's reply came after a few moments of silence, he said, "He agreed on some points but disagreed on others." Both the ladies looked at each other, and the perplexed Rakhi asked, "I don't understand what you have said just now. Please explain clearly."

Subhash Mukherji also felt the need to clarify the matter in detail. He started telling them, "When I insisted that my brother needed to be clear and tell me his views about Karan as a possible suitor for our daughter since both had started liking each other, he initially objected that Karan has no worth while assets. He is just doing a job. He then said that our daughter was used to a luxurious style of living. She has always had a big car, big house and lots of other facilities. I emphasized that both like each other and that Karan is well qualified and has a job in a multinational company, but he kept repeating that he is getting offers from very rich families and all the boys are well qualified. Then I requested him on behalf of Reena. This had some effect on him. He ultimately agreed but with a condition and said so very firmly that we should buy a good house for them, furnish it and give them all the necessary things like a big car, etc. I have no objection to his proposal. I felt quite happy that he ultimately agreed, but then I remembered Reena's remarks about Karan, that he is against accepting any dowry. I told him that his suggestion won't be possible as Karan is determined not to accept any dowry. He was surprised at first then told me that he would accept the proposal only if the boy accepts the dowry. I tried to explain that people like Karan are self-respecting individuals with a strong character, rarely found in our society, but he has his own logic. He feels money is more important than anything else. Moreover, he is of the view that Reena will be happy only if her husband has a good bank balance and all facilities. I had no choice but to accept his proposal. Now I shall try to convince Karan to accept what he is offered in marriage along with our daughter."

Rakhi said, "I think Karan should be ready to accept what *Dada* has suggested."

Reena said emphatically, "I know he will never agree." But she felt that there was no use discussing the matter with her parents.

The next day Reena got up in a gloomy mood. Even in college, she remained subdued all day. She passed her time half-heartedly. In the evening she rang Gayatri Devi to tell her about her uncle's decision. Gayatri heard it with calmness and said, "My dear, sweet Reena please don't lose heart. I shall try to convince your parents about Karan."

"But Grandma my parents are already convinced. It is my uncle who needs to be convinced."

"Don't worry dear, I will talk to your uncle but before that let me speak to your parents." Reena kept quiet. Gayatri said,

"Dear I will come to your house in a day or two and try to sort out the matter."

She only told Premnath that she was going to meet Reena's mother. She wanted to resolve the problem at her own level and if not then she would not be hesitating in taking his brother's help. She did not lose heart so easily and she considered Karan and Reena possibly an ideal couple.

Reena had already told her parents that Karan's grandmother wanted to visit them to discuss the situation.

Gayatri Devi went to Reena's house after confirming that her father was there. Subhash Mukherji showed his helplessness if Karan refused to acceptthe dowry. He explained that he and his wife were happy about Reena and Karan and admired Karan for not accepting dowry. They were happy to accept such an ideal young man as their son-in-law, but his elder brother would have to be convinced, as he could not decide against his brother's wishes.

The matter was now very clear to Gayatri Devi. She asked Subhash Mukherji to come with her to discuss the matter with his elder brother. The arrival of the unexpected guest perplexed Subodh Mukherji, but he showed his respect to her. Subhash explained the purpose of her visit. Subodh felt immediately that it was his responsibility to explain his stand on marriage. After giving the same arguments he had given to his brother, he requested Gayatri Devi to ask her grandson to accept the dowry as it was a genuine gesture from the girl's side. Gayatri felt that Subodh's condition was reasonable as far as they were concerned. He also conveyed to her that he was doing that only for his niece's future happiness as she was as dear to him as his own daughter. Ultimately the matter was kept pending until Karan's return from Mumbai. Both the brothers came to the gate to see Gayatri Devi off.

Gayatri Devi was in a fix. After dinner, she went straight to her bedroom and started thinking about the impasse. She did not speak to her brother yet, because she thought it would disturb his creative work. Moreover, a solution seemed possible only when Karan returned. She was impressed by the hospitality shown by Subodh Mukherji. His logic in favor of the dowry also seemed strong. Gayatri Devi, although an Arya Samajist, belonged to those strata of Indian society that considered dowry a normal custom. At the same time, she respected her grandson's ideals. Only Karan's arrival would solve the problem, she thought again. The last resort would be to hand over the matter to Premnath. If he did not resolve it also, then Karan and Reena would solve it in the best way they would. She prayed for a successful culmination of her grandson's affair and went to sleep.

In the morning, Gayatri thought of calling Karan, but she dropped the idea as it would unnecessarily disturb him. She preferred to wait and watch. If Karan called, she would just say that the matter was under serious consideration. In the evening she called Reena and assured her that she would try her best to sort out the matter.

It seemed to be the desire of all concerned not to express troubling thoughts to dear ones unless or until forced to. This notion was almost religiously followed by Gayatri Devi, Karan, and Reena.

Karan was desperate to know Reena's uncle's verdict. After assigning the job of inquiring and meeting Reena to his grandmother, Karan felt relieved to some extent. Two days before leaving Mumbai he thought of speaking to her to know the latest but decided against it as his repeated inquiries would unnecessarily make her anxious and in any case, he would be in Delhi with in the next two days.

The next day he called his grandmother and parents to say that he was returning within a day and did not mention Reena.

CHAPTER 28

Karan returned to Delhi on Saturday. He went straight to Ashok Vihar to meet his parents. He was sure he would not be able to meet Reena before Monday, so he called her and fixed a meeting for Monday evening at South Extension.

Both Malhotra families surrounded him to know more about his stay in Mumbai. He told them of his experiences, and they all ate together. After dinner, he opened his suitcase and distributed the gifts that he had brought for everyone. Later, when he was alone with his parents, his mother started enquiring about Reena and the next step. Karan clarified that the next step was to be taken after her uncle's consent and he explained the situation. Hisparents expressed their happiness that he liked a girl who was pleasant looking, well-mannered, and seemed good-natured.

On Sunday morning at Nath's farmhouse, after breakfast, both the sister and the brother were sitting in the drawing room when the phone rang.

Premnath picked up the phone and heard the voice of Vinod's uncle, Gopichand. He told Premnath that his brother's and Archana's families had met. They wanted to fix the date for the ring ceremony and wanted to know which dates would suit Premnath and Gayatri Devi, as they wanted their presence at the ceremony at Lucknow. Premnath after some deliberations replied that he would prefer to discuss this with Vinod and inform them accordingly in a day or two. He told Gayatri Devi about his conversation and called Vinod to apprize him as well. After some discussion, they decided that the date which would suit them was a fortnight later Sunday. Premnath asked Vinod to inform his uncle.

Gayatri Devi was waiting anxiously for Karan. As she knew Karan was coming back, she took care to fix the date to visit Lucknow not this Sunday but the one week onward. She wanted to keep herself and Premnath available at the farmhouse for the next few days to meet any exigencies concerned with Karan's affairs, which was making her quite anxious.

Karan's taxi entered the farmhouse and Sheru came to take the luggage to his room. Gayatri Devi heard a car come out of her room. Grandson and grandmother met in the hall. Karan bowed to touch her feet. Gayatri hugged him very affectionately. Both enquired about each other's health. Karan then asked, "Where is granduncle? I think he must be in the library as it is Sunday."

"No, he has gone to the Association meeting at Varma's." "When will he come back?"

"He may be back by tea time."

"Oh, I see. Where is Vinod then? He must be in his office."

"He went out to get the printer repaired."

"But Grandma today is Sunday."

"He said it is open today."

He then enquired about the staff at the farmhouse. He had already met the security guard, Sheru, Champa, and Shobha. After having a cup of tea he was thinking of asking about Reena when his grandmother said, "I talked to Reena the very next day you asked me to and invited her here."

"How is she?"

"She is quite well. I also went to her farmhouse and met her parents and uncle."

On hearing this, Karan's curiosity multiplied, but he kept silent waiting for his grandmother to speak. Gayatri did not like to keep her grandson waiting unnecessarily, so she informed him about her talk with Reena, her parents, and her uncle. Karan listened attentively, without interruption. When she stopped, she asked him, "What is your decision regarding dowry? Will you accept it as suggested by Reena's uncle?"

Karan understood very well that Reena's uncle was in no mood to give his acceptance until he was ready to accept the dowry. He replied after some moments of silence, "Grandma, there is absolutely no question of accepting the dowry." Karan's grandmother knew his grandson's views even then Karan felt that it was his responsibility to explain them in detail. He explained about the club and the oath they had taken. He also explained that they had taken such a course after thorough deliberations and that he was the leader of the group. Other members of the club, who had gotten married, fulfilled their promises of not accepting dowry, so he was totally committed to the cause.

Gayatri Devi knew about his views on dowry, bribery, the caste system, and futile rituals, etc., and also about his club, but she did not realize his strong commitment to these causes. She was impressed by what he told her but said nothing. Then Karan came to the topic more directly and said, "The time may even come when Reena has to take a decision against the wishes of her parents and uncle. I personally prefer to get their blessings. I don't see any objection from my family's side on this issue." Gayatri heard the out burst and said, "We are with you my dear son. My only worry is Reena. Dear son, what about your love for Reena? How can you put her in such a position and at the same time be so harsh on your own feelings toward her?"

Karan gave a smile, and replied, "My dear Grandma, Reena knows about my commitment. I also don't feel that she has any dearth of courage as she is also committed to love. A commitment to a higher cause, when in love, gives a lot of courage to the one who is committed."

I only wish to see you come through this impasse with flying colors," and she kissed her grandson on his forehead and asked him to freshen up if he wanted to, and come for lunch, which was ready.

Karan preferred to have lunch first so they went towards the dining table.

Just then Vinod entered the hall. He shook hands with Karan who congratulated him. Gayatri Devi spoke to Vinod, "Have you talked to your uncle?"

"Yes Grandma I talked to him and he will confirm the date after talking to Archana's parents."

"That's fine. We are just starting lunch, why not have it with us." Vinod and Karan were asking each other about the developments during the past three weeks. Vinod told him about Archana, and Karan spoke about his project. After lunch, Karan went to his room as he was a bit worried after what he had heard from his grandmother regarding Reena. He wanted to relax and think about the stalemate and the possible ways to solve it.

After entering his room he sat on a chair without thinking about anything.

Then he went to bed, but there was no sign of sleep. He got up within ten minutes and decided to go to the library. He preferred to sit at the rear where the sun was shining through the windows. He could see the beautiful pond, trees and flowers, and all those spots on the landscaped area around the pond; but Lover's Point where he had sat with Reena so many times was not visible. He recollected his granduncle's words that one could see people coming towards Lover's Point while sitting there but no one could see anybody sitting there. He had just accepted it, but that day he verified the fact. His mood suddenly changed as a result of recalling good memories and looking at nature's beauty while relaxing in the warmth of the winter sunshine. He gained some confidence and started evaluating the matter in a detached way. Reena's uncle was the only stumbling block. He was meeting Reena the next day, so he decided to tell her that he would like to meet him. Before that, he wanted Reena to meet him to show him her emotional involvement as well as her determination, so that the stumbling block may start weakening, and when he himself met her uncle, he would be ready to give way.

By the time Karan went downstairs for evening tea, his mood had changed. He saw his granduncle talking to his grandmother. He touched his feet and received his blessings. The old genius hugged him, and Karan responded with equal warmth. Premnath said, "How are you, young man?

When are both of my students becoming life partners?"

"Sir I am fine. Now I have returned and will see how to fulfill your wishes at an early date." Karan replied in a lighter vein, just to maintain a balance. He knew that things had turned against him and a lot of effort was needed from him to turn the tide. Gayatri also just smiled for the same reason.

Premnath changed the topic to inquire about his stay in Mumbai. During the next two hours, Karan spoke about his experiences in Mumbai, which Premnath heard with relish. He asked many questions about his project.

CHAPTER-29

It was Karan's first day at his office after his prolonged stay in Mumbai.

The company's senior management in Mumbai as well as that of the company for whom he had developed and implemented the project were very happy with his work. A letter of appreciation had already been sent to Delhi through e-mail.

He had just put down his briefcase when the peon entered and told him that the boss wanted to see him at once. He went immediately to Mr. Juneja's office. "Good morning, Sir, I was told that you wanted to see me."

"Hello Karan, how are you? Yes, I wanted to see you at once to convey the good news without delay." Karan showed his amazement. Juneja asked him to sit down and said, "Karan, accept my congratulations on two counts."

"Thank you, Sir, may I know..." Karan could not complete his sentence. His boss said, "First, on a letter of appreciation received from the Mumbai office for your work and secondly on your promotion." Karan expressed his gratitude to Mr. Juneja who accepted Karan's words by saying, "It's the result of your own hard work and sincere efforts. I am very happy that you will continue to work under me as in charge of the division with a manager's rank."

"That's wonderful Sir, I am really very happy to hear that you will continue to guide me."

He came back to his office quite pleased. He felt the impulse to inform his near and dear. He rang his father at the office, his mother at home, and his grandmother and granduncle at the farmhouse. They congratulated him and wished him further success. His grandmother added that there might be some delay, but no injustice would be done to Him. He easily understood what she wanted to convey.

At college, Reena was eagerly waiting for her meeting with Karan. She thought it would be crucial for deciding the course of their actions. She arrived well in time and in a few minutes, Karan was also there. They met after a long gap, with a lot of feelings but being a public place, they just shook hands. They went to their favorite restaurant, selected a quiet corner, and sat opposite each other. Karan gave the order to the waiter and instructed him to serve them after fifteen minutes.

Reena appraised him about her uncle's stand and questioned him after giving her own clarification, "I know your views very well about dowry, but even then I ask you to clarify the matter. Are you willing to compromise over the issue even a little bit?"

"I want to give you a detailed explanation. I developed these views to protect the honor of women, their feelings, and their natural human endeavors to choose their own life partners. Only since such criteria can the marriage institution become respectable."

"Yes, I know your feelings about women and I have full respect for that,but I again ask, will you compromise over the issue a little bit?"

"No dear, not at all, even though I love you so much."

"If my uncle remains rigid and my father follows his elder brother as an obligation then I can marry you against their wishes only."

The waiter served the order and Karan got time to think. He said, "You know I don't want that. I want our marriage to take place with the blessings of the family from both sides."

"You know Karan I never thought about such a drastic step until your grandmother showed her happiness at accepting me as her granddaughter-in-law. From the day we spoke, I started thinking about the possibility of such a step." Karan felt immense gratitude toward his grandmother who was playing such a constructive role. He felt the need to clear his position if there was no other way out. He said, "Dear Reena I may compromise, not on the dowry issue but on the issue of getting married against the wishes of your parents with a heavy heart, as a last resort."

"I am very happy to hear that. I can declare now with full confidence that though you are an idealist, you are not doing the thing in a dogmatic way rather keeping a pragmatic approach for finding out solutions to the typical problems."

"Thanks. Now let us try to solve the problem. I want to meet your uncle.""I don't think he will change his views."

"Even then I want to try my best."

"All right, I shall talk to my mother and inform you accordingly."

At the same time, the thought struck her that she would be in a better position to talk to her uncle. She also thought that a talk between her uncle and Karan could take some ugly turn resulting in offending the young idealist. When they were getting up she said, "I think I will meet my uncleand tell him whatever is on my mind without any inhibitions."

"This idea also came to my mind, and I think this may help our cause but Ilike to ask you will your strategy will bear any fruit?"

"My uncle loves me a lot. Perhaps on hearing my emotional out burst he may change his mind."

"If that happens really, it will be wonderful! I think you try it first."

It was decided that Reena would talk to her uncle, expressing her feelings for Karan. Reena was also determined to explain at length the difference between other young men and Karan. Suddenly Karan remembered his promotion, which, due to this emotional problem, he forgot to tell her. Reena was getting up as

Karan paid the bill, but he took her hand and asked her to keep sitting for a few minutes. He then said, "I forgot to tell you that I got a promotion today."

"Really! Congratulations! Karan this is very good and timely news. If God is willing this may help me in convincing my adamant uncle."

Reena was very happy. They got out of the restaurant and Karan went up to Reena's car. Before getting in she said, "All right, dear I shall try to talk to my uncle at the earliest possible opportunity and inform you accordingly."

When Karan reached the farmhouse and met his grandmother in the hall she embraced him and said, "Congratulations on your promotion, the news has lessened my anxieties about you."

"Oh Grandma, everything will be settled in a due course. Don't worry."

In a few minutes, Premnath and Vinod were there to congratulate him.

"Let's celebrate it with champagne,"

"I have it in stock. I bought some for Sulakshana's birthday," Premnath explained.

Premnath brought the bottle from his room and opened it in the name of Karan's promotion. Both Karan and Vinod were hesitating to drink champagne in front of Gayatri Devi, who, sensing it said, "This is a festive occasion, so I do not mind."

The three men took their glasses and Gayatri took a glass of juice. While sipping from his glass Premnath said, "When will we hear the next good news of your settling with Reena?"

"The matter is being discussed in the Mukherji's families. The decision is expected soon."

"Is there any chance of their disagreement? "I hope not."

Karan changed the topic and spoke to Vinod, "Now that your ring ceremony has been fixed. When are you getting married?"

"I feel both the families are quite keen to make it as early as possible."

That night Karan was wondering how Reena would talk to her uncle. The thought was going round and round in his mind. He let the thought come and go without any interference and after some time, sleep over powered him.

Karan had lunch in the company dining hall and came back to his office to relax, as it was still the lunch break. He sat on his chair and stretched his legs when his mobile rang. It was Reena. Her voice was subdued. She said, "Karan, I spoke to my uncle last night. In a nutshell, his response was negative."

Karan kept quiet. Reena started telling him the sequence "I explained to my uncle how well-placed you are in your job. I told him that you got a promotion even before completing two years in the company. I also explained to him that it was a rare quality in a young man not to accept dowry. And I also informed him how much I loved you." He listened patiently, and then said to me, "Dear I am receiving several offers for you. All the boys are either MBAs or engineers with MBA degrees." He further said, "There is one offer from an IAS officer's family. All are quite rich." He continued and said, "I don't respond to anyone due to your relationship and you know very well how much I love you and that is the only reason I have accepted your relationship with a very genuine concern and condition." Reena said at last, "You see he is so status conscious that even after getting impressed by your qualities he is not willing to accept our relations."

"Right dear, don't worry, I will do something."

In the evening when Karan came out of his office, he called Reena on her cell, "Reena, I still want to meet your uncle. Let me try to dispel his doubts."

"Yes, I also feel that we should keep on trying." "Yes. One should remain hopeful."

"We have no other way except to keep on trying. You also don't want togo ahead on your own."

With a smile on his face, he replied, "I feel the blessings of the families are very important on such occasions. Please remain confident."

"You are just worrying about me, where as I am ready for a second alternative."

"I appreciate your courage being a girl and ready to take such drasticaction, but I think you understand my reservations. As a last resort I am ready for it, but at present, let's wait and try."

CHAPTER 30

Karan entered the hall of the farmhouse and saw his grandmother and granduncle sipping tea. Gayatri Devi offered him a cup of tea, which he refused and made an excuse to go to his room. He was in a low mood. He decided to go to the library for a change of mood. He sat near the front window from where he could see the dimly lit garden. On the table in front of him were several magazines, but none attracted him. He just kept staring out side to distract himself from the negative thoughts. He read somewhere that 'when one stops worrying about something, one gets a number of creative ideas to solve the problem.' While he was trying to follow that concept, he heard foot steps and found that his granduncle was entering the library.

He said gently, "Karan dear, you seem a bit serious. Is there something you would like to share with us? Your grandmother is also worried about you." Karan thought about his elders who were worrying so much on his behalf. He decided at the spur of the moment to speak out and said meekly, "Sir I am worried about Reena."

"What's the problem? Please tell me without any hesitation."

"Reena's parents have agreed to our relationship, but her uncle does not. Her father's dilemma is that he can't give his permission without his elder brother's consent."

"But why does Reena's uncle not agree? What are his objections?"

Karan tried to explain Reena's uncle's objections, "He thinks I am without any worth while property which is a fact also. He wants not just a qualified bridegroom, but a rich one for his niece."

"But you have a good job."

"He is also insisting on certain conditions which I can't agree to." "What are those conditions?"

"He was told that I want to do a simple marriage and would not accept any dowry so his condition is that I must accept whatever they are going to offer in marriage, and only then he will give his consent."

"It's really a strange condition. How many young men in India refuse dowry these days? On the contrary, many of them demand or expect huge dowries."

"He says his niece has lived a lavish life and she will not be able to cope with a simpler lifestyle. The fact is that he himself is a very status-conscious person."

Premnath now understood the whole matter. "Let me see, how this matter can be solved," and placing his hand on Karan's back in a sympathetic gesture he went out of the library.

When he came back to the hall, he met his sister and said, "You were rightly worried. He is in a low mood."

"What's the reason for his low mood?"

"He told me that Reena's uncle does not agree to the marriage unless Karan accepts a dowry as it will enhance his financial status." Gayatri Devi was hoping that the matter would be resolved by Karan and Reena by convincing Reena'a uncle. She then realized that they could not resolve the matter. Premnath went to the telephone instrument leaving his sister engrossedin her thoughts. He spoke for about ten minutes to someone and after returning to his sister, he said, "I have spoken to Kamal Kapoor."

Gayatri Devi got puzzled, "Is there any reason that Kamal Kapoor should be concerned with our present stalemate regarding Karan? Or did you talk about something different?"

"It concerns Karan's present problem."

"How is Kamal Kapoor concerned with Karan's problem? I simply don't understand."

"If you remember we had both given Karan a gift of Rs. 21,000 on his eighteenth birthday? It was in 1993, I think."

"Yes, we gave him the gift which you had given to your friend to invest so that the investment could be given to Karan at the time of his marriage."

"It's simple. As Karan is getting married now, I talked with Kamal Kapoor."

"I don't understand how the present impasse can be resolved, and you have started preparing for his marriage!"

Premnath well understood his sister's curiosity, so he told her: "A few days ago when I was in Kamal Kapoor's office discussing the investments he told me that Karan's investments of INR 21,000/- has multiplied and is in a very good shape. I was quite busy with my own investment details, which were calculated and compiled for the Trust. That was my reason for going to his office. I did not ask him for other details. Now, after hearing that Reena's uncle thinks of him as a person without any substantial assets, I suddenly recollected Kamal Kapoor's remarks. I called Kapoor to ask him the exact worth of Karan's gift. Kapoor told me that he can't give the exact figure, but would tell me tomorrow."

Gayatri said, not particularly impressed, "Do you think Karan will become richer by a few thousand or a few lakhs."

"I don't know really but from Kapoor's hint I could say it must be a few lakhs."

"Thank God if it is so, but do you think a few lakhs in Karan's kitty will satisfy Reena's uncle?"

"Well, I can't say. I just want to wait and see. It was a small gift given by us on a special occasion, which was invested in his name with all documents properly signed by him. I know

Karan in any other eventualities he is not going to accept any money, even though I am always ready to help him on that count. Luckily in the present case money was invested in his name only."

"Yes, he has a lot of self-pride, particularly in money matters."

"That's why I can't solve his problem by simply transferring some of my properties in his name."

"But is it not a good quality about him?"

"Yes it is very good quality and I completely agree with him. He is a real gem. We should be proud of him." Premnath suggested that they should not speak to Karan about what Kapoor told them and wait for the next day to get the details. She agreed with her brother.

At dinner, Premnath started on the topic of landscaping and told the three listeners some of his interesting experiences. He picked on that topic just to avoid the grim atmosphere in the house.

It was a difficult night for Karan, but without losing heart he made hisplans to meet Subodh Mukherji and clear his wrong notions.

After breakfast as per Premnath's suggestion, they sat on the front lawns to discuss the family affairs. Only ten minutes had elapsed, when Sheru brought the cordless phone to Premnath. "Hello, Premnath speaking." Gayatri Devi noticed that her brother was listening with a sense of surprise in his eyes as well as on his face and only saying, "Oh I see! It's Wonderful! It's Unbelievable!" repeatedly. Her curiosity was aroused.

Premnath spoke for about half an hour and after giving the phone to Sheru he turned to her sister and said, "Oh my God! I simply can't believe what I have just heard!" He was looking very happy.

Her sister who was already desperate to know the details of the conversation said, "Why don't you tell me what has happened?

I can guess from your face and a few words which you have spoken on the phone that the news is very good."

"Yes, you are quite right my respected sister. The news is not only very good but fantastic and it's regarding Karan."

"Has Reena's uncle agreed?"

Without creating further suspense Premnath said, "The call was from Kamal Kapoor, and do you know what he said?" He continued speaking and informed Gayatri Devi that Karan's money was invested by him about seven years ago in the shares of Infosys Technologies in the same year when its shares were just out in the market after its IPO was floated. That money had multiplied to more than two crores (twenty million) Indian rupees.

Gayatri Devi was dumbstruck. After about a minute Premnath heard, "If what you have said is really true then I can say only that God is merciful!"

They decided to tell Karan only after telling Reena and her parents. They felt that now the matter could be discussed with Reena's uncle in a new light.

She rang Reena's house and informed her mother that she and her brother would be coming to their house to discuss the affair in the light of some new developments.

At about 5 p.m. Premnath and Gayatri Devi went to Mukherji's farmhouse.

Rakhi and Reena were eagerly waiting for them. They were sitting on their front lawn. After the initial pleasantries, Rakhi said with a touch of eagerness, "What is the new development? I also informed Reena's father who will be coming any moment."

Premnath took the matter into his hands, told the ladies about the development briefly, and concluded that Karan was a millionaire. Both the ladies heard Premnath with bated breath. Signs of astonishment and happiness came to their faces.

Reena could not stop crying from uncontrolled joy. Gayatri got up and embraced her. There was the sound of the main gate opening and Subhash Mukherji appeared in his car. In the next few moments, he was with his guests and invited them into the main building so that they could discuss the matter over tea in the drawing room. Rakhi requested Premnath to repeat what he had just told them. Subhash Mukherji was also surprised to discover that Karan was a millionaire. The news gave him immense happiness and he said, "We, both wanted Karan to be our son-in-law, but as you know there was a hitch from my brother's side which I couldn't ignore."

On that Gayatri Devi said, "Now I think his objection will be over as Karan has his own assets."

"Surely now he should not object. I shall talk to him as soon as he comes from the office." He said beaming.

Sweets, tea, and snacks were served. Everyone was very happy. Premnath cracked a few jokes with his student. Gayatri Devi told the Mukherjis that they had not informed Karan yet and would be telling him only after getting the green signal from their side. After tea, they took their leave. Reena also dropped the idea of congratulating Karan on becoming rich.

Karan did not come home even at 7 p.m. A telephone rang in Nath's farmhouse and Premnath, who was waiting for a call from the Mukherji's house, picked up the phone. It was Karan informing him that he would come home around nine, as there was a meeting in the office. Premnath had to make an extra effort not to tell Karan the news. Both the sister and the brother were walking up and down the hall anxiously without talking. The telephone rang again but it was not the Mukherjis, it was kamini. After greeting each other Premnath, gave the phone to his sister. Gayatri Devi felt the urge to tell kamini the good news but cutting the story short she told her everything in ten minutes. She asked kamini to tell Vijay, Ramesh, and Sunanda but warned her that nobody would speak with Karan till the time they get the green signal from the Mukherji's house, which was expected at any time. Gayatri put the family at Ashok Vihar in an extra state of excitement with her news. When the phone rang again, both said, "Now this must be Mukherji." But it was Karan's father inquiring about his son's riches. Though everyone was perplexed, they were very happy also. After satisfying him, he said that his mother would talk to him later as she was busy. Their wait was becoming more difficult. At 8 p.m. the phone rang once again, and this time it was Subhash Mukherji. He told Premnath excitedly that his elder brother had given his consent. Premnath expressed his happiness and gave the phone to his sister so that she could hear such good news directly. Gayatri's joy was beyond bounds. She also spoke to Rakhi and Reena and told Reena that Karan was attending a meeting in his office and would be coming late. She was so overwhelmed with joy that she wanted Reena to be near her at that very moment. Reena's parents did not find any problem with the request and agreed to send Reena with her maid to Nath's farmhouse. Within half an hour Reena was sitting with Gayatri and Premnath enjoying and sharing the happiness with her tutor and would-be grandmother-in-law.

At about 9 p.m. Karan entered the hall and found his grandmother and granduncle talking to Reena. He was utterly surprised to see Reena there at this hour. All the three greeted him who was at a loss. His bewilderment was cut short by Premnath. He told him the details about his riches. Karan gave a broad smile but remained calm. His grandmother informed him, "Now Reena's uncle is ready to see you as her husband."

"Oh, that's fantastic! Grandma, why did not you tell me earlier?"

"Because this news was linked with the first news of you're becoming arich man."

Now Premnath entered the discussion and said, "Karan you will never change. You are not so excited to hear that you have more than two crores worth of liquid assets. You do seem excited about knowing that you are going to be Reena's husband. I really appreciate your reaction."

At Gayatri's request, they all went to the dining table for dinner. When they sat down, Karan asked his granduncle, "Where is Vinod?"

"He has gone to his parents for two days for the preparation regarding his engagement."

After dinner, Gayatri asked Reena to come with her mother the next day in the evening so that they could discuss the engagement date. Reena shyly replied, "All right, Grandma." Karan went with Reena and her maid up to the gate of their farmhouse.

He was busy for the next hour or so talking to his parents, sister, uncle, aunt, and cousins. Gayatri invited them to the farmhouse, and it was decided to meet on Saturday.

The next day Gayatri asked Karan to come early so that his engagement date could be discussed, and he would be able to meet Reena. Karan only gave a smile to her. Reena came with her mother well in time. Karan arrived fifteen minutes later. Rakhi and Gayatri were discussing the possible date of the engagement. Gayatri asked Karan to take Reena for a walk in the garden. Both of them went happily, thanking the grand lady in their hearts. Karan took Reena to his favorite spot, Lover's Point. As soon as they reached there they embraced each other. They remained thus for about ten minutes, while they kissed each other. Their faces were red, and after overpowering their emotions, they returned.

Gayatri Devi said that their engagement date would be finalized in the presence of Karan's parents and that Reena's parents were also coming on Saturday to meet them. Karan said, "Saturday is fine, as on Sunday I have to attend my club meeting."

His grandmother laughed and said, "I will see how many club meetings you will be attending after your marriage." The others also laughed. After tea, Karan went up to

Mukherji's gate to see the Ladies off.

Epilogue

After attending the birthday party at Sagar's and meeting again both the families at Nath's and Mukherji's, Karan was driving his car toward his Villa at DLF phase-1 Gurgaon where he had shifted last year after getting his house constructed with his father's technical know-how and supervision.

There he purchased a plot of 500 sq. yards when he got the money after selling his part investment in Infosys Company shares before his marriage. He also purchased a three-bedroom flat at Vasant Kunj where he moved immediately after his marriage. He asked his parents to shift from Ashok Vihar to Vasant Kunj, but they preferred to continue staying at Ashok Vihar. At the beginning of 2006, his father became chief engineer from the post of director which previously he held. His sister Mudra after doing her engineering at Indraprastha University, Delhi, joined American Company as a software developer in their office at Neta Ji Subhash Place, Pitampura. Karan's company 'Prime Mover' shifted its office from Bhika Ji Cama Place, New Delhi to Gurgaon last year. That was the reason he also moved to Gurgaon. Reena's uncle who was the main hurdle in their marriage now seemed quite satisfied with Karan's new prosperity and style of living.

As it was Saturday, so everybody insisted on both Nath's and Mukherji's farmhouses that they stay for Saturday night, but Reena explained to them that there would be a meeting of the club on Sunday at their house in Gurgaon. About 20 men and a few of Karan's friend's spouses were expected to come. There would be a lunch arrangement although the cooks were already arranged. Karan after dinner came to his study to prepare for the next day's meeting.

Their club ran very well. They also set up an NGO and got it registered in 2001. NGO did a lot of commendable work in mobilizing Delhi and surrounding NCR people to know their rights and to fight all kinds of irregularities and administrative high-handedness of the authority. He prepared a speech for the following day and started visualizing the progress of the club and NGO. He was becoming an important person whose articles were regularly appearing in different newspapers which also helped him in his mission of public awakening. He was sure of his views that India's progress had slowed down miserably owing to rampant corruption prevailing in government departments which affected the quality of life of its citizens.

He was certain that once people realized the malaise of corruption, they would uproot it without delay by penalizing directly the corrupt elements in people's court.

In the mean time, Reena also came to study after Sia went to bed. Sia wasborn last year after about three and half years of their marriage. She inherited the features and complexion of her parents. That's why she was a very attractive child. These days she grasped the new words very quickly.

She was already calling *Mama, Papa, Dada, Dadi, Bhua, Nana, Nani.* Now she started speaking difficult words like Bubbles and Mobiles etc. and kept repeating them a number of times during the day. She imitated her grandmother and grandfather very well for the way they took their medicine and gargled.

Reena after completing her MA in French from JNU joined a language job in an MNC which she left when Sia was born. Now she was doing French translation work at her house in her free time to keep in touch with the language.

The moment Karan became free from his thinking and started looking athis wife, he could not resist saying to her, "I don't know Reena how everybody in the family likes you so much.

What magic do you have? Let me know."

"There was no magic." Reena said smilingly and continued, "When I gotmarried to you, I accepted every member of your family as my family member. I gave them respect and due regard. That's all and that is my only magic."

"I feel jealous sometimes when my parents or grandma or even granduncle like you so much and are always worried about you."

"Why do you say that? My parents even consider you as their elder son." For the younger son, it was understood to be Reena's younger brother Sumit, who after doing his MBA, joined his father and uncle's export business.

"Am I not?" Both laughed over it. Karan came towards Reena and hugged her and for the next moment, they were ecstatic.

www.ingramcontent.com/pod-product-compliance
Lightning Source LLC
Chambersburg PA
CBHW020329160726
47992CB00004B/1766